AN AVALON ROMANCE

A NEW ATTITUDE
Debby Mayne

Former wild child Denise Carson has settled down a bit—with her own bookstore she has learned about responsibility. Then one day, Andrew Mitchell walks into her store with his sister to shop. He has lived most of his life amidst the blue blood of Nashville, until he gets a job with a gift wrap manufacturing plant in Clearview.

His sister Amy, wanting to get away from the shelter of their over-protective parents, goes against their wishes and joins him. Denise sees the potential in the shy and withdrawn girl and sets out on a mission to help her spread her wings.

Naturally, Andrew resists. After all, Amy is his little sister, and she's been placed in his care. He takes his job of protecting his sister seriously, but Denise is determined to continue working on Amy. When her "experiments" start taking effect and Amy starts blossoming, Andrew disapproves more and more.

The only problem for Denise are her feelings for Andrew—can she be her spontaneous self and help those she cares about without alienating him and his conservative ways?

A NEW ATTITUDE

•

Debby Mayne

AVALON BOOKS
NEW YORK

Library of Congress Catalog Card Number: 00-107007
ISBN 0-8034-9455-6

Published by Thomas Bouregy & Co., Inc.
160 Madison Avenue, New York, NY 10016

PRINTED IN THE UNITED STATES OF AMERICA
ON ACID-FREE PAPER
BY HADDON CRAFTSMEN, BLOOMSBURG, PENNSYLVANIA

This book is dedicated to every woman who
has overcome life's obstacles,
learned to stand on her own two feet and
feel good about who she is.

Many thanks to editors Erin Cartwright and Mira Son
for reading my manuscripts and offering
enthusiastic words of encouragement.

I thank my dad Jeff Tisdale for teaching me
some of life's most important lessons,
such as how to fix a leaky faucet and basic carpentry skills—
things every woman should know.

Thanks to Wally, Alison and Lauren
for all the smiles and laughter that brighten
each and every day of my life.

Chapter One

"You're cute as a little button," Denise Carson cooed to the baby in her arms. "Ya know that?"

Baby Emily grinned up at her caregiver, that toothless, bubble-filled smile warming the entire room. Then, she gurgled back at Denise.

With a deep sigh, Denise had to swallow. She'd never imagined how intense her maternal feelings would be once she held a tiny baby in her arms, warm against her chest.

"I have to put you down, sweetie," Denise said as she gently placed the baby in the portable crib she'd set up in the back room of her bookstore.

Emily looked at Denise for a moment, then turned and began to examine her fist before shoving it into her tiny mouth. She almost seemed to understand.

The bells on the door jangled, letting Denise know there was a customer in the store. She dropped a kiss on the baby's face, then turned and headed for the shopping area.

"May I help you?" she asked, approaching a couple she'd never seen before.

The man looked to be somewhere around thirty, while the woman with him appeared much younger. They exchanged a glance, then turned back to her and smiled.

"I'm looking for something stimulating to read," the man said, his voice soft but guarded. "Perhaps something inspirational."

Denise smiled at the couple and nodded toward the edge of the store. "We have an entire section devoted to inspirational books," she said. "I'm sure you can find something that will please you." She directed her gaze to the woman. "And is there something you'd like to look at?"

The woman just shrugged and looked at the man. He faced Denise and smiled back at her. "She likes the same thing I like."

"Oh," Denise said, pulling back a few steps. She got the distinct impression they didn't want to be bothered, but she wasn't the type to stand back and let a new person come to town without some sort of friendly gesture on her part. Sucking in a deep breath and extending her right hand, she walked toward them and said, "I'm Denise Carson, owner of Carson's Bookstore. I don't believe we've met."

The man appeared startled at first, but he quickly recovered. He took Denise's hand in his and nodded. "Andrew Mitchell."

Denise glanced at the woman and crinkled her forehead. "And you are . . . ?"

The woman nervously replied, "Amy Mitchell."

Oh, Denise thought. So they were married. A couple. Well, wasn't everyone these days? Everyone but her, she amended.

Forcing the smile to remain on her lips, Denise backed away, the lump in her throat growing larger. "Nice to meet you, Amy and Andrew Mitchell. I hope you find your visit to Clearview to be a pleasant one."

"Oh, we're not visiting," Andrew said as he placed his hand in the small of Amy's back and began to guide her to the section Denise had pointed out. "We're moving here."

Denise's eyebrows shot up. "You are?"

Amy and Andrew both nodded. Andrew chuckled. "Yes. We've just bought a house in Allendale."

"Oh," Denise said, feeling a catch in her throat. Allendale was the section of town where she grew up. A neighborhood that was filled with big, old houses and people who had more money than they could ever spend in a lifetime. Amy and Andrew Mitchell must be well-to-do. "What brings you to Clearview?" As if that was any of her business.

"Swetson's Gift Wrap," he replied. "I'm the national marketing director."

Denise forced a smile. Swetson's was the newest of the many manufacturing firms that had recently moved to Clearview. She'd been on the committee to attract more clean business to town, so she was well aware of the company.

"I hope you like our little town," she said, taking another step back. "We have friendly people and great schools, so I'm sure it won't take long for the two of you to feel connected."

Andrew and Amy exchanged another glance, then looked back at her. "No," he said, "I'm sure it won't take long at all."

Denise retreated further as the couple headed over to the inspirational section, whispering softly to each other. She found herself longing for a relationship like that, one where she could share a few words with someone who was a part of her. But it seemed that all she'd ever have was this bookstore, so she might as well be grateful for that. It was more than she'd had a couple years ago, when she was still searching for what she wanted to do with her life.

Clearview had been a sleepy little town for so long that it took everyone by surprise when Denise stormed into her teenage years. She'd met her best friend Bethany by then, and the two of them had raised so much ruckus their elders threatened to keep them from hanging out together. However, their friendship was so strong, nothing could keep them away from each other. Denise had to smile to herself as she remembered some of their escapades.

Bethany had moved to town with her mother after her parents divorced. They'd gone back to the two-story monstrosity of a house at the end of a quiet cul-de-sac, the one Bethany's grandmother Gertie Chalmers had insisted on keeping even after her own daughter was grown. "Good thing," Denise's parents said at the time, "because now they have Bethany living there, and they need all that space for her to test her wings."

When Denise first met quiet Bethany, she knew all it would take was a gentle nudge to bring out her personality. Well, she was the only person in town who wasn't surprised when Bethany's personality nearly matched her own.

After college, Bethany had decided not to return to Clearview. Instead she'd gone to the big city of Atlanta and gotten a job with a large accounting firm. Obviously, it wasn't what she really wanted because as soon as Gertie had her stroke, Bethany quit her job and moved back to Clearview.

The old house had sold to the new preacher in town, which Denise knew bugged Bethany out of her mind when she first met him. She had to chuckle at the thought of Reverend David Hadaway and Bethany Moore getting together. It seemed so unlikely, but it had happened. And now, Bethany was right back in that old house, married to the nice preacher, and being a wonderful mom to Emily and a fabulous aunt to David's nephew Jonathan. In fact, it seemed to Denise that David and Bethany had Jonathan more than his own parents did.

Suddenly, the shrill sound of a baby's wail startled Denise from her thoughts. She raced to the back room and scooped Emily into her arms. Emily's high-pitched scream stopped momentarily, and she let out a few shaky sobs. Then, she started all over again.

Denise checked Emily's diaper, then held her up over her shoulder, patting her back. But Emily still screamed.

A voice came from the door. "You might try the 'football hold,' " Andrew said.

"Football hold?" Denise asked. What in the world was that?

"Yeah," he replied, reaching for the baby. Denise pulled Emily back, so Andrew stopped. She wasn't about to let some stranger hold her best friend's baby, even if she *did* know his name and where he worked. He placed the book he was holding in his arms like he was holding a football to demonstrate. "That used to work for me."

"I-I'll give it a try," Denise said, shifting Emily to the position he was showing. Almost immediately, Emily stopped her shrieking cries. Denise grinned up at Andrew. "Hey, thanks."

He grinned back at her and gave her a mock salute. "No problem." Then he disappeared.

Denise stood there and gently swayed from side to side as she thought about the man who'd just shown her a new trick to make babies stop crying. He and Amy must have kids, she thought.

She tried putting Emily back in the crib several times, but each time she did, Emily let out an ear-piercing scream. With a sigh, she decided to keep the baby with her. After all, Denise was the owner of this store. She could do anything she wanted. Although she'd had the place for a couple years now, she still delighted in the fact that she was a business owner. Who woulda thought?

Denise headed out to the front section of the store where several more customers had come in. There were a couple of elderly women in the fiction section, and a young man perused the aisles she'd filled with various types of reference books. It felt good to know that so many people in Clearview enjoyed books as much as she did.

Finally, Andrew and Amy came to the cash register with their selections. "I'll take these," he said as he plopped three in-depth non-fiction inspirational books on the counter. "And my sister will take these." He added her books to his stack.

"Y-your sister?" Denise said, her gaze going back and forth between Andrew and Amy. She didn't make a move to ring up the books.

Andrew chuckled. "Of course, she's my sister," he said as he glanced down at Amy. "What did you th . . ." Suddenly, the dawning of recognition showed on his face. "Oh, I'm sorry. I didn't make it clear. My sister moved here with me since I didn't know anyone."

Amy grinned and Denise felt the heat rise to her cheeks. She felt like a total idiot. She shrugged. "Not that it's any of my business," she said, trying hard to cover for her blunder. And hopefully, he wouldn't notice how pleased she was that Amy wasn't his wife.

Andrew chuckled, then stopped as their gazes locked. Denise felt the scrutiny of his eyes as he studied her for a moment. It was almost as if time stood still. "That's quite all right, Mrs. Carson. I can understand how you'd come to a different conclusion."

Amy nudged him in the side with her elbow, as if she found the very thought offensive. Denise giggled, and Andrew laughed out loud. This time, the joke included her. Her spirits lifted instantly.

Almost as suddenly as the mood had lightened, Andrew's face became guarded. He pointed to the baby Denise was still holding. "Cute kid."

Denise nodded. "Yes, she *is* adorable, isn't she?" Now, it dawned on her what they must be thinking. She held the baby up for them to get a good look. "Emily is my best friend's baby. Isn't she sweet? Well, at least she is when she's not screaming bloody murder. My friend's husband is a pastor, and they had to go out of town to a religious retreat this morning." After a brief pause, she added, "And that's *Miss* Carson. I'm not married." The instant she said that, Denise felt like kicking her own backside. She must have sounded pretty desperate to have come out with that comment.

Amy's eyes darted back and forth between her brother and Denise, at first in amusement, then in guarded concern. "Andrew," she said softly. "We really need to go. The moving van should be here in an hour, and I still have a few things to do before they arrive."

Andrew glanced down at his watch and nodded. "That's right. We really need to get back."

Denise felt her heart singing the whole time she rang up their purchases. The new guy in town sure was a cutie, she thought. And as nice as anyone she'd ever met, too.

The second they left, Emily pulled her head up from Denise's arm and looked her in the eye, almost as if to ask where Andrew and Amy had gone. Denise kissed the baby on the forehead and winked at her. "You take after your mom and me, darlin'. You know a good-lookin' guy when you see one, don't you?"

Emily grinned and gurgled. Denise hugged her close and felt a warmth spread through her body. Things were definitely looking up right now.

Somehow, Denise managed to hold onto Emily while she took care of all her customers. She didn't want to put her down and risk having her ear-splitting cries hurt business. Besides, it felt wonderful and warm to hold Emily close to her heart, especially now that she felt positively giddy. Maybe nothing would ever happen between her and Andrew Mitchell, but it sure did feel nice knowing there was hope. A few dates, and she'd probably be cured of any silly childish dreams and romantic thoughts. But until then, she could dream.

All morning, Denise felt like singing. Her senses were sharper, and her heart felt like it would burst with pleasure, all because she'd just met a new man. Years ago, she would have taken it in stride, since she was the self-proclaimed greeting committee in Clearview. But things had changed. She'd become more grounded and responsible, which sometimes prevented her from flitting about like she once had in social situations. She spent more time at home, going over books for her business, and she tried to keep her social life down to a dull roar. Even though she knew this life was right for her now, there were things she missed about knowing the business of every single person in town.

Andrew seemed like a really cool guy, but one thing disturbed her. His sister Amy, although pleasant enough, seemed nervous and scared.

Denise found herself thinking about Andrew and Amy for the next couple of hours. Now that she knew they were brother and sister, she could see the resemblance. But while Andrew was handsome and very sure of himself, Amy seemed to retreat into herself. She had some pretty features, but she didn't play them up. Instead, she went without any makeup that Denise could see, and she wore clothes that were all wrong for her. With features like Amy's she could definitely carry more color and get away with it.

Denise rolled her eyes at her own thoughts. There she went again, thinking about fixing other people's lives. She should have learned her lesson by now, after all the trouble she'd gotten herself into in her past.

But then, it sometimes worked out, didn't it? Look at how happy Bethany and David were. Didn't she have a hand in that happy union?

Come to think of it, she'd had more successes than failures in her own meddlesome days. She'd been responsible for several matches that wound up in marriage. And she'd taken Bethany from the depths of despair after Bethany's parents' divorce and helped her learn to enjoy life. Maybe she'd just have to take Amy Mitchell under her wing and teach her a little bit about making the most of her good features.

And then, there was Andrew. The bonus to becoming friends with Amy was that she'd get to see the new hunk . . . er, nice man in town. Hopefully, he wasn't spoken for by another woman. Denise hadn't seen anyone she was all that interested in since she'd bought the store.

Emily seemed pretty happy for the rest of the time Denise had her in the store. Bethany had told her she and David would be back late afternoon, but she came through the bookstore doors around two o'clock.

"You're back already?" Denise asked, unable to hide her disappointment. She loved having Emily to herself when she wasn't crying, but now she had to give her up.

Bethany shrugged, a huge grin spreading across her lips when Emily spotted her. Both mother and baby held their arms out, and Denise felt a familiar tug at her heart. It must be nice to have so much mutual adoration.

"How'd she do?" Bethany asked.

Denise shrugged. "Before or after the fire?"

"Wha—?" Bethany squinted and glanced nervously around the store. "Fire?"

"Well, after the thieves left . . ." she cut her words off when she noticed the stricken look on Bethany's face. "Everything was just fine, Bethany."

Bethany placed her hand on her chest. "Don't scare me like that."

Denise shook her head. "Do you think I'd hang around here after something like that happened? Really, Bethany."

"I know," Bethany said. "Besides, I trust you completely with my child. Did she cry much?"

Denise started to lie and say that Emily had been perfect, but she thought better of it. "Well, just a little bit this morning, but Andrew Mitchell showed me how to get her to stop."

One of Bethany's eyebrows shot up. "Andrew Mitchell?"

Feeling her face heat up once again, Denise nodded. "He's new in town."

"Oh," Bethany said, nodding in understanding. "Good looking, too, huh?"

"Well," Denise said, her voice rising an octave. "Yes."

With a giggle, Bethany shook her head. "You always were a sucker for a hunky guy. Did you manage to get any of his statistics?"

Denise waved her hand to brush off that comment. "I don't do that anymore, Bethany. That's so juvenile."

Bethany folded her arms across her chest and glared at her. "Okay, Denise, spill it. Tell me about this Andrew Mitchell."

Without wasting another second, Denise leaned over the counter, her arms folded, her eyes lit up with excitement. "He's about six feet tall, dark brown hair, and very well built. He bought a house in Allendale, and his sister moved here with him. Their furniture is being delivered today."

"No," Bethany said after a brief pause. "I don't suppose you did anything so juvenile as get his statistics." Denise could tell her friend was trying hard to stifle a smile. "Did you find out where he's from?"

"Of course not," Denise said indignantly. "That would be nosy."

Bethany cracked up. "Yes, I suppose it would." She took Emily and walked toward the door. "Maybe after you get to know this Andrew guy a little better, you can invite him over to the house. I'd like to meet him."

Denise sniffed the air, acting like she wasn't fazed in the least by Bethany's interest. "We'll see." She sighed. "Don't keep Emily away from me so long next time. I'm afraid she'll forget who I am."

"Don't worry about that," Bethany replied. "Emily loves her Aunt Denise."

As soon as Bethany and Emily were gone, Denise started moving around the shop, dusting everything, then straightening books. She had more energy than she'd had in a long time, and she almost didn't know what to do with herself. Good thing Bethany had taken over her bookkeeping, or she'd have to concentrate tonight, something she knew would be extremely difficult to do now.

Denise closed the shop at six and headed for her car. The last thing she expected was to run into the new people she'd met this morning. But when she heard a sweet female voice, she knew exactly who it was without having to look up.

"You close early?" Amy said. "Most of the shops where we came from stay open at least until nine."

Denise cleared her throat. She felt the need to defend Clearview, but she didn't want to upset a new friend. "The malls stay open late, but downtown pretty much rolls up at six." She glanced around Amy and saw that the woman was alone.

"He's back at the house," Amy said. "I'm here looking for a few things we're still missing."

Denise hadn't meant to be so obvious. "Oh, that's fine. I understand. I just moved into my own house a couple years ago myself." She paused for a moment before adding, "Whatcha lookin' for? Maybe I can loan it to you."

Amy suddenly got a horrified look on her face. "Oh, no, I'd never borrow something from a stranger."

Denise chuckled, now that she realized she had the upper hand. "I'm not a stranger anymore, Amy. We met this morning, and around here, that makes you my friend."

Nodding, Amy appeared slightly confused. Denise could tell she was trying to act like she understood, and that endeared her. "We can't seem to find any light bulbs. I figured there would be a store around here that might have some." She winced. "And the pots and pans are somewhere in the boxes marked 'kitchen,' but I forgot to write on the outside what was in each box." She continued to look at Denise apologetically, like she was causing trouble and didn't want to. "There must be at least two dozen 'kitchen' boxes."

Denise reached out and took Amy by the arm. "Come on, Amy, we're going to my house. I buy light bulbs by the case, and I have some pots and pans you can borrow."

"Are you sure?" Amy asked, not resisting in the least.

"I'm positive," Denise replied. "I might even have some leftovers you can bring home and heat up. I made soup last night, and I have a huge bowl left over."

"Sounds good," Amy said shyly.

"Hey, why don't you follow me to my house? It's not far."

Amy's face fell. "Uh, Denise, I don't drive."

"How did you get here, then?" Denise asked, glancing around to see if Andrew was nearby.

"Andrew dropped me off. He said he'd pick me up in half an hour."

"Any way you can get ahold of him? I'll take you to my house to get the things you need, then I can drive you home."

Amy's expression grew pensive, then she pulled out a cell phone. She spoke softly, and Denise couldn't hear much of the conversation. Amy nodded as she flipped the phone to a closed position. "All set. Andrew said it would be fine for you to bring me home."

They got into Denise's car and headed for the neighborhood of tiny, older homes not far from Allendale. "How do you like Clearview?"

Amy shrugged as she kept her eyes focused outside the car. "So far it seems pretty nice."

Denise got out and went around behind her car to

walk to the door with Amy. "It's not very big, but it's home."

Amy flipped her long brown hair over her shoulder and took a quick glance at the house. "It's so pretty. I love what you did with flowers."

A narrow line of pink and white flowers bordered the front of the house, while there were clusters of yellow, red, and purple flowers in scattered beds around trees and throughout the yard. The front door was flanked on both sides by large terra cotta pots filled with red salvia and white petunias that draped over the edges.

"I like color," Denise stated as she searched through her mass of keys, pulling out the one that unlocked the front door. "It cheers me up."

On the edge of a sigh, Amy nodded. "Yes, color does tend to do that, doesn't it?"

Denise tilted her head to one side and took a long look at her new friend, wondering what it was she'd heard in Amy's voice. It sounded like wistfulness, but she wasn't sure.

Chapter Two

"Oh, wow!" Amy exclaimed as she walked through the house Denise had bought a couple years ago and updated. "Look at all this."

With a chuckle, Denise said, "I told you I like color."

"I've never seen anything like it," Amy said, her eyes wide and her mouth forming a circle.

With a shrug, Denise pulled off her jacket and took Amy's. "Most people would never think of painting a living room wall yellow, but since it's my favorite color, I figured, why not? It cheers me up."

"It's beautiful, Denise!"

"Thank you, Amy." Denise continued walking toward the back of the house to the kitchen. "Let me see if I can find an extra set of pots and pans you can use until you find yours."

"Oh, but I don't want to impose on you."

Denise waved her off. "Don't worry about it. I can only use one set at a time, and they're just sitting in the cupboard collecting dust." She pulled out a stainless-steel pot and pan, then went on a search for the lids. As soon as she found them, she opened her refrigerator door, pulled out a plastic container, and slammed the door with her knee. "Let me put some soup in that pot, so all you have to do is stick it on the stove and heat it up. Do you need bowls?"

Amy shook her head as she stood there in amazement. "We found the bowls and plates."

"Good. At least you can eat cereal for breakfast."

"I never dreamed you'd be so generous, loaning us your perfectly good pots and pans, Denise. What can we do to repay you?"

Denise felt very uncomfortable now. She wasn't used to people thanking her over and over and even offering to pay her, and she didn't like it. "People in small towns do this sort of thing for each other. I'm sure everything will work out in the end. You'll do something for a new neighbor, and they'll do something for someone else. Good deeds don't always have to boomerang right back to where they came from."

Amy nodded as she just stood there, holding the pot of soup. "I never really thought about it like that, but you're right."

"Let me get some light bulbs," Denise said, turning her back. "They're right here in the closet."

As they walked to the front door, Denise grabbed Amy's coat and helped her by holding the soup while she put it on. "Where are you from, Amy?"

At first, Amy looked guarded, but then she must have realized she was safe. "Nashville."

Denise squinted. "I like Nashville. It's almost a big city, but it has small-town ways."

"Yes," Amy agreed. "But people aren't nearly as open there as they are here."

"Really?" Denise had never thought of anyone being any different from people in Clearview, regardless of where they were from. "I used to go there when I was a little girl, and I thought the people were pretty friendly."

"Friendly, yes. Open, no." They headed outside and stood beside Denise's car. "For the most part, people there just stick to themselves unless they want something."

"I'm sure they're not all like that," Denise said with a smile as she helped Amy with her things. "You have nice people everywhere."

"I guess so," Amy said as she slid into the passenger seat. "But my parents kept close tabs on me, so I didn't get to discover much of anything outside the little world they created for me."

Denise had no idea what Amy was talking about, but she didn't want to pry or push any more than she already had. It was time to take Amy home, so she ran around to the driver's side and slid in behind the wheel.

The Allendale section wasn't very far from where she lived, but it might as well have been on the other side of the world as far as Denise was concerned. People who lived in those stately old mansions had no idea how it felt to have to live paycheck to paycheck, something Denise discovered after she got out into the real world. Sure, her parents had left her plenty of money, but it didn't come in one huge chunk. It had been set aside in a trust fund, thank goodness, or Denise would have already spent the whole thing by now and had nothing to show for it. As it was, she had enough to start the business, and each year, she was able to pay off a little bit more of her mortgage on the cottage. Her father had been smart to plan things the way he had, but she hadn't thought so at first.

Denise wondered how Andrew and Amy had been able to purchase a house in Allendale. The houses in that neighborhood started well above what was considered affordable, by any standards. And although she'd heard that Swetson's salaries were much higher than average, she knew that they didn't pay enough for any of their employees to live there. Andrew and Amy must have come into money some other way.

Amy was quiet all the way home. Denise could tell she was like a sponge, absorbing all the newness of life around her. As Amy got out, Denise said, "Need help with those things?"

Amy glanced nervously over her shoulder. "Uh, no, I think I can get everything." She looped her bag with the light bulbs over one arm, picked up the pot of soup, and held it against her chest, while Denise handed her the other pan that had a loop she dangled from her finger. "Thanks again, Denise," she said before she scurried inside her house.

As soon as Denise got back home and inside her little house, the phone rang. It was Bethany.

"Hey, Denise, I've been thinking . . ." She paused.

Denise groaned. "That could be dangerous, Bethany. Better stop doing that."

Ignoring her friend's comment, Bethany said, "Why don't you invite your new friends over for dinner this weekend?"

"Uh, I'm not sure."

"Oh, come on, Denise. This isn't like you at all."

Denise studied her nails. When she was a teenager, she would have run straight to her best friend and begged her to meet the really cool guy she'd just met. But she wasn't a teenager. She was a responsible adult. Her hopes for her future were different now. "I shouldn't have told you about them."

"Uh, Denise," Bethany began, "I have a confession to make."

"A confession?"

"Yes. I heard all about the Mitchells from someone else."

"Yeah, I suppose you would have."

"Wanna know what else I heard?" Bethany said. "I heard he's not only single, he's very good looking."

"That's an understatement," Denise said, no longer able to control her enthusiasm. So much for acting like a responsible adult. That would have to come later, after she and Bethany discussed everything about Andrew Mitchell. "Uh, who else did you talk to about the new people?"

"David," Bethany said bluntly.

"He told you Andrew was good looking? I didn't know men noticed things like that about other guys."

"They don't," Bethany said with a giggle. "But I asked him what he thought, and he said you'd probably like the way Andrew looked."

"Why didn't you tell me?" Denise squeaked.

"So, how about dinner?" Bethany said with a chuckle in her voice, ignoring Denise's last question. "David said they hesitated when he first asked them, but they sounded relieved to know someone."

"Is there anything else you're not telling me? Like did you meet them?" Denise asked, her voice still squeaking with the excitement she couldn't tone down.

"No, but David told me all about them. And they're planning to come to church on Sunday."

"They go to church?"

"Yes, and they want to get active in some of the charity work we do, too."

Denise's heart felt as if it might leap out of her mouth. "Did David find out where they came from?"

"David said something about Nashville, but I don't know for sure."

"Yes, that's right," Denise said. "Did you know they bought a house in Allendale?"

"No!" Bethany exclaimed. "I wonder how they managed that!"

"That's what bugs me," Denise said in a conspiratorial whisper. "I'm thinking they must be involved in something on the side. Maybe even something illegal."

Bethany laughed. "Come on, Denise. Don't talk about your old neighborhood like that. Your dad was an honest businessman, and he was able to afford it."

"Yeah, but he owned the bank. He got stock options and other perks normal people don't get. We're not talking that kind of thing for mid-level management with Swetson's."

"How do you know he's mid-level management?" Bethany asked.

"Well, I-I don't," Denise stuttered. "But I would think that being marketing director of a gift wrap company would be mid-level management."

On the edge of a sigh, Bethany agreed. "You're probably right. I'm sure there's a logical explanation for their being able to live there. Besides, it's really none of our business." She hesitated for a moment before adding, "At least now it isn't. Try to hold your imagination back this time, Denise."

Denise managed to get off the phone quickly after that. Bethany had been her best friend for many years, but she wanted to think about Andrew on her own, without Bethany's common sense dampening her own vivid daydreams. She wanted to imagine something exciting, something filled with danger, something way out of the ordinary that would enable Andrew and Amy to be able to buy a house in Allendale.

The next morning, Denise hopped out of bed before the alarm clock rang. She'd been restless all night, so she figured she might as well get started on her day. She had to gather her ledger books so Bethany could work her weekly magic on them.

Ever since she'd turned over the bookkeeping to her best friend, business seemed to soar. Bethany's suggestions of how to invest and handle inventory control were brilliant, and they more than made up for the bookkeeping fee.

This was the morning when children and their moms would be lined up outside the store when she arrived. Before she even opened the store, she had an hour devoted to telling stories and reading books to the preschool set. That, she figured, was the closest she'd ever get to having kids.

What she hadn't counted on was seeing Amy out front waiting with all the other people. Denise greeted all the familiar half-pint customers, then turned her attention to her new friend. "How was the soup?"

Amy beamed. "It was terrific, Denise. I didn't know you had story time in the store. Need help?"

At first, Denise started to say no, but she caught herself. Maybe this was what Amy needed in order to feel connected. "Sure, I could always use an extra pair of hands."

As soon as she had all the children seated in a circle, Denise held up one of her favorite children's books and told them the name of the story as well as the author. A couple of kids raised their hands to ask a question, and she answered them patiently. Amy stood off to one side, watching the whole thing.

After she read the story, Amy waved to get Denise's attention. "Excuse me a second, kids. I need to talk to Miss Carson for a second."

She carefully stepped past the children as she walked toward Amy. "I was wondering . . . well, if you don't mind . . . I sort of like reading books to kids, and . . ."

Denise's eyebrows shot up. "Would you like to do the next story?"

Amy nodded. "I'd love to, that is, if you don't mind."

"No, of course not," Denise said in amazement. "I don't mind at all."

"Hey, kiddos, this is Miss Amy. She's gonna read

the next story to you, and I expect you to treat her just like you treat me."

All the kids said, "Hi, Miss Amy," and she smiled and greeted them in return. Within minutes, she had them spellbound by the story Denise had pre-selected the day before. She was very good with children, something that surprised Denise.

At the end of the story hour, after Denise and Amy had taken turns reading aloud, the moms retrieved their children and made their purchases. One of the benefits to mothers during this hour was that they got to look at books and shop while their children were being entertained. Denise considered it a win-win situation, where everyone benefited. She always rang up quite a few sales after the story hour.

The children and their mothers left the store with smiles on their faces, and Amy lingered behind. She and Denise stood beside the cash register, waving goodbye to everyone.

The second they were alone, Denise turned to Amy and said, "Want some tea?"

Amy began to shake her head no, then thought better of it. "Sure, I'd love some."

"Be right back."

A few minutes later, Denise came from the back room carrying two steaming hot mugs and handed one of them to the other woman. "I'm glad you came by early this morning, but I'll bet you were caught by surprise."

"Yes," Amy said, nodding, "but I wouldn't have missed it for anything. Those children were adorable."

Denise chuckled over a sip of tea. "Sometimes they are, but not always. I have a feeling they were on their best behavior for you."

Amy sipped her tea, then stopped and stared off into space. Denise had the distinct impression that she'd come to talk with her about something, but she was afraid to start.

"Is there something I can do for you, Amy?" Denise finally blurted out. She wasn't one who hesitated very long when she wanted to know something.

Amy sighed. "Well, sort of."

"Okay." Denise set her mug on the counter and leaned over her arms. "Why don't you tell me?"

After swallowing, Amy turned to Denise and offered a shaky smile. "I-I'm not sure how to ask you this, but Andrew told me I should just do it."

"Andrew's right," Denise said. Where was he, anyway? She'd have to ask Amy after they discussed this other thing.

"We moved here because of Andrew's job, but I don't have a place to work yet," Amy blurted out.

"What do you do?" Denise had helped people find work many times, so she was used to this kind of question.

With a shrug, Amy said, "That's just it. I don't know how to do much of anything."

"Oh, come on," Denise said with a chuckle. "I just

watched you in action with those children. You have a way with the younger set. Have you ever thought about working in day care?"

Amy crinkled her nose. "I don't think I'd like that."

"No," Denise said, staring off toward the other side of the book store. Suddenly, an idea dawned on her. The person she'd hired part-time when she first opened told her she was thinking about staying home with her grandchildren. Maybe Amy would want to help out around the store. Denise actually needed someone who could work more hours so she could get a few personal things done.

"I've got an idea, but I can't say anything yet until I talk to one of my employees," Denise said with excitement. "I'll give her a call in a few minutes and see what she says. Why don't you stop by later this afternoon, and we can talk then?"

Amy grinned. "If you're not too busy."

"If you come around three, I'm generally not busy then."

"Okay," Amy said as she backed toward the door. "I'll go help Andrew unpack, then I'll get him to bring me. I think he wants to get another book."

Denise's heart jumped at the thought of seeing Andrew again. It was almost like he'd disappeared once he left her store the one and only time she'd seen him.

After Denise called her employee, time seemed to drag until three o'clock. Right when the minute hand was straight up, Amy walked through the front door of the bookstore. Denise leaned to the side to see if Andrew was with her, but she was disappointed to see that Amy was alone.

"You wanted to talk to me?" Amy asked, pulling Denise's attention to where it should have been.

"How would you like to work here at the book store?" Denise didn't believe in playing games, so she just blurted it out.

"I-I'd love it!" Amy said. "But are you sure? I mean, don't you already have plenty of help?"

"Well, I did, but one of my part-timers said she was thinking about staying home. I called her and asked if she was serious, and she was relieved I'd found someone."

"That sounds wonderful!" Amy's happiness was evident, and Denise was glad she'd taken a big chance like she had.

They discussed hours and pay for the next few minutes. "I wish I could offer you more, but I'm just a small business. If you ever need time off, just let me know, and I'll cover for you."

"It's perfect for me," Amy said. "And I'm sure my parents will approve."

That was the first Denise had heard about their parents. "Your parents . . . are they still in Nashville?"

Amy nodded and cast her gaze downward. "Yes, and they weren't thrilled about me moving here with Andrew."

"Why did you come?" Denise couldn't stand it any longer. She was dying to find out.

"Andrew didn't know anyone here, and I felt like it was time to move out, so when the opportunity presented itself, I just did it. At first, my dad was mad, but Andrew promised to watch over me."

"I think you'll be happy here," Denise said, still wanting to know more but understanding that the timing wasn't right to keep prying.

Just then the bells on the door made their jingling sound. It was Andrew.

Denise had to catch her breath to keep from losing it. As he walked in, she saw that he was even better looking than what she'd remembered. She self-consciously straightened her hair.

He grinned at his sister. "Ready to go back to the house, Amy?"

"Yes," she said on the edge of a giggle. "You're not going to believe this, Andrew, but Denise and I have been talking . . ."

Andrew looked at Denise, still smiling, and nodded. "Hi, there, Miss Carson. My sister seems to have taken a liking to you and your store."

Amy cast a conspiratorial glance toward Denise, then looked back at her brother. "I've got a job, Andrew."

"You what?" he said, his voice coming a little louder and stronger than before. "Where?"

Denise stepped forward. She had no idea what was

going on between this brother and sister, but she felt an overwhelming need to protect Amy. "I've offered her a job working here."

Andrew took a step back and looked back and forth between Amy and Denise, then he glanced around the store, as if he were inspecting it to see if it was good enough for his sister. Then he narrowed his eyes and focused on Denise. "Are you sure about this?"

Denise folded her arms over her chest and stared right back at Andrew. "I'm positive. She's excellent with children. In fact, I think I might turn the children's hour over to her after she gets used to things around here."

"I guess it'll be okay," he said after a brief pause. "I'm just a little surprised you actually came out and asked her."

"You told me I should," Amy said.

"I know, but I didn't think—" He glanced at Denise and clamped his jaw shut.

"I like this store, and I want to work here." Amy spoke in a little girl voice, unlike how she'd talked when it was just her and Denise.

"You can tell me about it later," Andrew said. "The phone company is coming late today, and we need to get back."

Amy joined Andrew and walked toward the door. "When did you want me to start, Denise?"

Denise glanced at both of them before replying. "As

soon as you can pull yourself away from the move. Do you want to come in sometime this week?"

Andrew took Amy by the arm and said, "She'll call you."

Then, they left. Denise stood there in amazement at what had just happened, unsure now of whether she liked Andrew or if it had just been an initial physical attraction based on looks. Right now, she didn't much care for the way he'd acted when he'd found out about Amy's new job, although she could tell he knew Amy was going to ask about it.

Amy was a grown woman, so why couldn't she work wherever she wanted to? Why did Andrew have to discuss it with her?

She got her answer later that afternoon when Bethany stopped by. It was nice to have someone to talk to, someone who understood how she felt about things.

"It's my understanding that Amy has always been sheltered by an overbearing father," Bethany said. "Andrew voiced his concern to David when they first met."

"But that still doesn't explain why he treats her like a little girl," Denise argued.

With a shrug, Bethany said, "I'm not sure, but I don't think Amy has ever had a job."

"You're kidding," Denise said with a drawl. Both she and Bethany used to take summer jobs so they'd have their own money to spend as they pleased. Besides, her dad told her it was good for her to have the responsibility of having someplace to be at a certain time.

"No," Bethany said, shaking her head. "And I have a feeling Andrew is feeling more like a parent than a brother right now. I'm sure that can be pretty overwhelming to a single guy."

Denise thought for a moment. "So that explains it." She sighed. "Maybe I should have spoken with him first."

Bethany reached out and patted Denise's shoulder. "I think you did the right thing. Like you said, Amy is a grown woman. When you offered her the job, you probably made her day."

"I'm sure of that." Denise chuckled. "You should have seen how she lit up."

"I can imagine." Bethany pulled the ledger from beneath the counter and added it to her stack of books. "I'll work on this tonight and bring it back tomorrow. From what I've seen, business is good for you, Denise. I'm proud of you."

Denise gave a bittersweet smile. "I wish my dad could have seen me be successful at something. He was always so worried about me. Even though he never said it, I'm sure he was afraid I'd make a huge mess of my life."

"I don't think so," Bethany said. "I'm sure he realized you'd find your way and do something constructive."

"At least I don't have to live off the trust he set up." Denise gulped. "But it sure does help to have it during lean business times."

"You would have done just fine without it, though," Bethany said thoughtfully. "You've got a natural mind for business." She backed toward the door and stopped. "I almost forgot. We're having some people over for dinner on Friday night, and I wanted to make sure you could come."

"Of course, I can," Denise said. "You don't think I'd pass up a free meal, do you?" She cast her gaze downward. "Will the Mitchells be there?"

With a chuckle, Bethany replied, "Of course. Since it didn't look like you'd cooperate by asking them yourself, I took the bull by the horns." As an afterthought, she added, "I've invited Nana, too."

"That should be interesting," Denise said.

"Very interesting." With that, Bethany left, and Denise stood there staring at the door. This had been a very interesting day.

When Denise got home from work that evening, the light on her answering machine was blinking. It was Amy, telling her that she'd be at the store first thing in the morning. And she added that her brother would be there with her. He wanted to discuss a few things with Denise before he let her work there.

For some reason, that last part of the message bugged Denise all the way to her toes. Why did Andrew have to discuss anything with her? Why didn't he let Denise and Amy work things out? Did he think she was going to take advantage of his little sister? That really burned her up.

All night, Denise tossed and turned, feeling her anger as it seeped into every thought she had. Even counting sheep wouldn't work because their little woolly faces kept looking at her with suspicion.

By the time she got to the store the next morning, Denise was ready for battle. Amy wasn't there yet, so she unlocked the door, went inside, and put her things in the back room.

When she came back out, both Amy and Andrew were there waiting for her. Amy looked excited about getting started, but Andrew was guarded. The look on his face told her he was *not* happy about something. She must have said something, but for the life of her, she couldn't figure out what it was.

Chapter Three

"Amy, would you like to start right now?" Denise asked guardedly. She really didn't want to make Andrew mad. She darted her eyes over to see his reaction.

Nodding, Andrew motioned toward his sister. "Go ahead if you really want to do this."

"Really?" Amy said, her voice shrill with excitement. She turned to Denise and said, "What would you like for me to do first?"

With a lump in her throat, Denise said, "Why don't you walk around and straighten the shelves. I normally do it before I leave each day, but I was in a hurry to get out of here last night, so I didn't do it."

"Sure," Amy said as she backed away and began to move around the store, doing exactly what Denise had told her to do.

"You do realize this is my sister's first job, don't you?" Andrew said as soon as his sister was out of earshot.

"You're kidding," Denise said. Naturally, she didn't mention that Bethany had already told her. "How old is she?"

"Twenty-three." His voice cracked. Denise could tell this was a difficult moment for him.

"Twenty-three and never had a job?" Denise still couldn't believe it. "How did she make a living before you moved here, then?"

With a shrug, Andrew replied, "My parents didn't think it was important for her to get a job right away. After she finished college, she moved back in with them and just did the social things that are expected of high society Nashville girls."

Denise's eyebrows shot up. "She's a college graduate?" Her mind raced. What in the world was Amy doing, asking for a clerk's job in a bookstore when she could do so much better?

"Yes," Andrew said with a sarcastic chuckle. "I know what you're thinking, but things are obviously different here in Clearview. Back where I come from, in the social circle I was raised in, girls went to college, got their liberal arts degrees, then sat back and waited for a husband."

"And she didn't have any prospects, huh?" Denise asked.

"To the contrary," he stated flatly. "There were

plenty of eligible men my parents approved of, but none Amy liked. So when I got my job here, she begged me to let her come with me."

"Oh," Denise said, nodding in understanding. The only way their parents would approve of her leaving the cushy nest they'd provided was for her to be in the care of her doting brother. "I think I understand now."

Andrew crinkled his forehead as he continued. "And I can't be too careful because if things don't go well for her, my parents will make her move back to Nashville."

"How can they make her do anything?" Denise asked. "She's an adult."

He tilted his head back and snorted. "They have their ways."

"Purse strings, huh?" Denise remembered how her wealthy friends' parents dangled the purse strings in front of them, using money to get their sons and daughters to do their bidding. Fortunately, her father didn't do that, but it was probably because he'd earned his own way in life, being one of the rare first-generation wealthy in Clearview.

"You got it," he said with a nod. "Besides, I really love my little sister, and I don't want to take any chances with her."

"Did your parents ever try to hold you back from doing what you wanted by offering money?" Denise asked, unable to keep her nose to herself. She couldn't help wondering, and the words just came out.

"Of course," he said. "But I never much cared for their money."

Denise narrowed her eyes and licked her lips. "And I suppose the house in Allendale was something you earned?"

Andrew glared at her for a moment, his gaze hard and cool, but then it softened. "I suppose I should take offense at that comment, but I'll choose not to. No, that house in Allendale was definitely *not* something I earned. In fact, it's not even my house. It's Amy's."

"Amy's house?" Denise asked, stunned that an employee of her bookstore could own a house in that neighborhood.

He let out a labored sigh. "That was the only way we could convince our parents to let her come here without a fight. They had their people look for a suitable home for their princess."

Denise heard the sarcasm in his voice, but she let it drop. She was certain she'd find out more later, and now wasn't a good time to go into family problems. At least not when she had a new employee to train.

"Well, thanks for letting her work here, Andrew," Denise said with compassion. Although she'd never experienced firsthand what they were going through, she was aware of how some wealthy parents manipulated their children with hefty bank accounts. And

Amy was so desperate to get away, she was willing to agree to any terms to get what she wanted.

With a sincere grin, Andrew nodded and winked at his sister. "I think this will work out just fine."

Denise let out a sigh of relief. She didn't realize she felt uncomfortable about being under such close scrutiny, but she was happy he approved. It meant a lot to her.

"I'll take care of her," Denise said. "I promise."

He paused for a moment. "The best thing I can do as a brother at this point is teach her how to take care of herself. And I'd appreciate it if you'd treat her like you would any other employee."

"No problem," Denise said flippantly, contrary to how she felt. She was more than slightly confused, though, because he seemed to want to protect her on one hand, and on the other hand he wanted Amy to learn her way in the world. He was acting amazingly like many parents she'd known. Andrew had taken on a very heavy responsibility, and he didn't want to mess anything up. That was sweet, but Denise knew he was probably overwhelmed at the task.

After he left, Denise gave Amy a list of jobs to do, mostly to familiarize her with the store. In her experience of hiring people, it was best to have them moving around, getting used to the sections and understanding what their customers needed before she put them on the cash register.

When things slowed down, Denise motioned for

Amy to join her for a cup of tea, something she did to give herself a breather when she had the chance. "You're doing a great job, Amy."

"Really?" Amy wasn't able to conceal her pleasure at the compliment. Then her shoulders slumped. "I guess Andrew told you this is my first job." She looked almost as if she might cry.

Denise reached out and touched Amy's arm reassuringly. "We've all got to start somewhere." She hesitated for a moment before she decided to go ahead and tell Amy about her own childhood. "Did I tell you I grew up in Allendale?"

Amy's head jerked around, and she stared openly at Denise. "No, you never mentioned that. Are your parents still there?"

"No," Denise said sadly. "They both died a few years ago."

"I-I'm sorry," Amy said as she cast her gaze downward.

"I am, too." Denise felt a sigh of sadness travel through her body. By the time it got to her lips, it came out in a whoosh. "My dad would have been so proud of me now. He never saw my store."

"I'll bet your dad was proud of you, anyway," Amy said in childlike wonder.

Denise shook her head. "I doubt it. I caused my parents so much grief, they didn't know what to do with me."

"I can't imagine," Amy said, shaking her head. "You seem like such a responsible citizen."

"That only came when I had to make it on my own."

"They didn't leave you the house?" Amy asked, her inquisitive nature getting the best of her. Denise thought it was cute that Amy was asking so many questions that probably didn't agree with how she'd been brought up. People with her social standing were taught early on that you didn't pry. They found out things about others, but it was done in a more discreet way.

"The house was added to my trust fund. My dad stipulated that I'd get it once I reached a certain age. But his attorney suggested I sell it instead, since I had no desire to move back in."

"Really?" Amy said. "Why not?"

"You might not understand this now, Amy, but after I managed to purchase my cottage, I found something out about myself that I never want to let go of."

"What's that?" Amy stood there, her hands folded primly on the counter, more telling than she probably realized of her class and her finesse.

"I learned that I could make it on my own and that it doesn't take a mansion or elaborate furnishings to make me happy. All I need is honesty and self-respect, and now that I have that, I'm just as content as I'll ever be." Denise left out the part about wishing for a man to share her life with. That would be too much for Amy to hear now, especially since she was already experiencing so many new things at the moment. Besides, Denise wondered if having a man in her life would complicate things for her. She had everything exactly like she wanted it.

"I wish I had your courage," Amy said on the edge of a whisper.

"You do," Denise replied as she moved away from the counter to help the customer who just walked in. "You just haven't found it yet. This job is a good start, though."

Denise had to keep her distance from Amy for the rest of the morning. She wanted to let her new employee process all the new information without too much interference. But it was hard, since she was curious about Andrew, and she knew Amy held some answers to her questions.

At noon, the door opened, and Andrew walked inside. Denise could almost feel his presence, but it was Amy's eyes that gave away the fact that he was in the store. Her face actually lit up when she saw him coming.

"How's my baby sister doing?" he asked Denise as he got closer to the cash register. "I never did find out what time you went to lunch."

Denise turned to Amy, determined to treat the young woman as an adult rather than talk to Andrew about her like she was a child who needed a report from the teacher. "You did a nice job today, Amy. Why don't you take the afternoon off and come back in the morning? There's a reading group from one of the retirement centers that comes in here, and I thought you might like to get to know some of them."

Amy glanced nervously at her brother, then back at Denise. "Are you sure you don't need me this afternoon? I really don't mind if you do."

At first, Denise started to tell her she wasn't needed, but then she thought better of it. She lifted her finger to her cheek and squinted. "Come to think of it, I could use you for a couple hours. You're pretty good with the children's books. A few teachers dropped off their required reading lists last week, and I think tomorrow's the deadline to have the books. Most kids like to wait until the last minute."

Denise watched Amy as she glanced at Andrew, almost like she was asking his permission. He shrugged. "She's your boss, Amy. Better do what she tells you."

With a huge self-satisfied smile, Amy turned back to Denise and said, "I'll be here, then. What time?"

Denise glanced at the wall clock, ignoring Andrew's wink in her direction. Her heart was fluttering. "The kids won't be getting out of school for another couple of hours, so you can take a long lunch break. If you're back by two-thirty, we can start pulling some of the books so they won't have to hunt for them."

Amy nodded as she grabbed her coat and followed Andrew out the door. He glanced over his shoulder and mouthed a thanks to Denise. She was amazed at how much responsibility he'd taken upon himself, yet he managed to do it with grace.

After they left, the store seemed very quiet and dark all of a sudden. Although Amy had no working experience, she caught on quickly, and she was very smart. Denise could tell she'd been sheltered, but that was okay. Being in the real world of business would provide plenty of the lessons she'd need to get by.

The usual lunch crowd came in and browsed, a few of them purchasing bestsellers like they always did. Then it got very quiet again, which was good. Denise used that time to heat up some water for a cup of tea, which had become her usual morning and afternoon routine. It kept her from feeling too harried, and it gave her something to look forward to.

She was almost finished with her tea when Andrew and Amy came back. Denise handed her new employee a list of books to pull, pointed her in the right direction, and said, "Just get three or four of each, and we can pile them in stacks behind the counter."

Andrew leaned against the counter as he watched his sister do her job. As soon as she was far enough away not to hear him, he said, "She really loves books. Thank you for being so generous and offering her a chance to do something constructive with her time."

Denise gulped. Andrew was acting like she was doing them a favor, when Amy had actually wound up being a blessing to her instead. "I'm really not being all that generous. One of my employees just gave her notice recently, and I was wondering what I'd do. I'm already working too many hours as it is."

He chuckled. "I'm sure you didn't figure on having to train someone so fresh and young."

Denise bristled at his comment. He sounded way too condescending toward his sister. No wonder she was having such a hard time getting out in the world. "I've had younger employees before. Amy catches on very quickly. She's a smart *woman*." Denise emphasized to get her point across to Andrew.

"I didn't mean it that way, Denise." He pursed his lips and watched Amy for a moment, then turned and faced her again. "What time should I pick her up?"

Denise inhaled deeply. "Don't bother picking her up. I can bring her home when we close."

Andrew narrowed his eyes, making Denise think she might have a battle on her hands. For some reason, she felt like she was having to pass some sort of test as his baby sister's first employer.

Why was it that when she wasn't anywhere near Andrew she could fantasize about being romantically involved with him, yet when they were in the same room, she was so unsure of what he was thinking? Was he being defensive because he didn't trust her? Denise wanted to shake him and tell him to let his sister make decisions on her own. But of course, she didn't. She couldn't. That was Amy's job.

As the children filed through the front door with their parents after school let out, Denise showed Amy what to do. Then she stepped back and let Amy take over. Amy did a fantastic job, making Denise proud. Too bad Andrew hadn't stuck around to see his sister in action. She was an excellent bookseller.

The parents seemed to like Amy, too, because by the time they'd paid for their purchases, they were chatting with her like she was their oldest friend in the world. Time flew, and before Denise realized how late it was, Amy pointed to the clock.

"Do we have to leave right at six?" Amy asked.

"Yes," Denise replied, grabbing her keys and heading for the front door to lock up. "If we stay open later, people will expect it all the time."

"Oh," Amy said, a hint of sadness on the edge of her voice.

"Are you having fun?"

Amy clasped her hands together like a little girl at a surprise birthday party. "I'm having the best time, Denise. This job is absolutely perfect for me."

With a chuckle, Denise said, "I wonder if you'll still be saying that when you get your first paycheck."

They put everything away, counted the money, and made out the daily deposit to put in the bank night drop. "Ready?" Denise held the back door for Amy.

As Denise drove to her old neighborhood, nostalgia went through her. She turned onto the main street that led to all the smaller lanes of the place where she grew up. As the feelings flooded her veins, she cleared her throat to make small talk so she wouldn't think too much about the parents she missed so much.

Denise chuckled. "So you're the couple who bought Old Man Hensley's house."

"You knew Henry Hensley?" Amy asked. "I thought he died a long time ago."

"He did, but his memory still lives." Denise smiled as she remembered the time she and Bethany rolled Old Man Hensley's front yard. They had a tough time throwing the toilet paper all the way up some of those huge trees, but somehow they managed. And the next day, they went back to admire their handiwork.

"I heard he didn't have any children, and the house was tied up in all sorts of litigation before we bought it," Amy said. "It's a nice house, but the kitchen could use a little work."

"Really?" Denise felt a pang of excitement over the prospect of renovating a kitchen. That was one of the things she'd thoroughly enjoyed about buying her cottage.

Amy nodded. "It's dark and dreary, the total opposite of your kitchen. There's dark wood everywhere, all the way from the floors and cabinets, to the paneling on the walls."

"Wood-paneled kitchen walls?" Denise stopped herself from making the comment she was thinking. From what she remembered, quite a few houses in this neighborhood were paneled throughout—not because the inhabitants thought it was pretty, but because it gave the impression of old money. Her own mother had painted white walls with a pretty floral border in the kitchen, something that had appalled some of the people who dared visit the new family on the block. She smiled.

"What's so funny?" Amy asked as Denise pulled into the driveway of Old Man Hensley's old house.

"I was just thinking . . ." Her voice trailed off as she thought about whether or not she should make the offer. Should she? Her first instinct was to forget about it, but then it would be so much fun. "I was just thinking," she began again, "that we could brighten up the kitchen quite a bit with some paint and a trip to the wallpaper store."

Amy's face brightened, then it fell. "I've never done this kind of thing before."

"I can help you." Denise chewed on her bottom lip for a few seconds as excitement grew inside her. Not only would she have fun with the decorating, she'd get to see Andrew. That was the most exciting part about this whole plan.

"You'd do that for me?" Amy studied her for a moment, leaving Denise feeling like she was under scrutiny for something she'd done wrong.

Denise shrugged. "Only if you want me to. I don't want to stick my nose where it doesn't belong." *Please let me help*, she wanted to beg, but she didn't.

Amy clasped her hands beneath her chin. "I'd love to do that, Denise." She looked around at the house that stood before them like a huge, looming monster. "This house isn't something I would have chosen to live in, to be honest with you."

"Andrew picked it out?" Denise asked.

"No, he hates it, too. My dad insisted I live in a place like this. Otherwise, he wouldn't agree to the move." Amy pursed her lips and squinted. Denise thought she saw a little moisture in Amy's eyes, but she didn't say anything. "He's very protective toward me."

Denise nodded. "I understand." She glanced at the house and shuddered. The place sure did bring back a lot of old memories. She and Bethany had made up horror stories about things they imagined happening behind those stone walls, none of them based on truth but on what they conjectured. "But in spite of its dark dreary walls, we can make it into a doll house." She inhaled and blew out a huge breath before adding, "A very big doll house."

Amy giggled. Just then the front door opened, and they both looked up to see Andrew standing there. "My brother is worried about me, too."

"He needs to lighten up," Denise said before she had a chance to think. She wanted to hit herself. Why couldn't she keep her big mouth shut and not say so much of what she thought?

"Andrew's nothing compared to my dad. Now that's someone to reckon with."

"I understand." Denise had to bite her lip to keep her side of the conversation from sounding judgmental. She didn't want to push Amy out of the car, but for some reason, the young woman was reluctant to get out. She just sat there making conversation, even now that Andrew was obviously growing impatient.

"You said you grew up in this neighborhood," Amy went on. "Did your dad make you feel like you were in a fortress with a moat around it?"

Why had she asked Denise that? Denise had already sensed that Amy had been held back from the world. Did Amy think everyone who came from money was like that? And how much would Andrew give in to Amy learning to be more independent? He'd told Denise that he wanted her to learn how to make it on her own, but she wasn't sure he meant it the same way she took it.

"There were times," Denise began very carefully, "when I thought it would be fun to live in a small cottage with a picket fence, like a lot of the other kids I knew did."

"Yeah, that's exactly how I felt," Amy said, her voice high-pitched. "But my dad would never let me get away with doing some of the things I've thought about doing. Did your father keep you from experiencing life just to protect you?"

As much as Denise wanted to come out and ask questions, she knew better. Based on how Amy and Andrew were acting, there were some things they obviously didn't discuss. Denise had always been very open, but she knew some people were uncomfortable with that. She'd have to take her time and observe. Maybe she could help.

Chapter Four

Denise finally managed a chuckle. "No, but not that he didn't try. Let's just say that I was somewhat of a rebellious child. If he'd tried a stunt like that, I would have figured out a way to make it come back and bite him on the—" She stopped herself before she resorted to giving the young woman ideas. It had been a long time since she'd been called a "bad influence" on a friend. She didn't want to resurrect that reputation at this time in her life.

Amy cast a glance toward her brother and sighed. "I guess I'd better go in before Andrew has a conniption."

Denise sat and waited until Amy was safely up the sidewalk and almost to the front door before she started to back out. But she stopped when she spotted

Andrew jogging out toward her car, motioning for her to wait.

She pushed the button and lowered the car window. "She did a great job today," Denise told him, figuring that was what he wanted to discuss.

He nodded absentmindedly. "I'm sure. But that's not what I wanted to discuss with you, Denise." Andrew shoved his hands in his pockets and studied her, not saying anything.

"Well," she said impatiently. "What *did* you want to discuss?"

Andrew glanced up at the sky and then back at Denise. "I was kind of . . . well, kind of wondering . . ."

Squinting her eyes at Andrew, Denise tilted her head to one side. "You were wondering?"

He squared his jaw and nodded. "Yes, I was wondering if you'd like to have dinner with me some evening." After a brief pause, he added, "That is, if you're not seeing anyone regularly."

Andrew's proper manner of speech mixed with his discomfort endeared him to her heart once again. While he tried to play the part of protective older brother, probably more to take over his father's role than anything else, he now came across as a softy who was sensitive to women. Denise had been around enough men in her life to know when someone was a jerk, and Andrew definitely wasn't one of those, she knew now for certain.

She grinned from ear to ear, almost involuntarily.

"I'd love to go out to dinner with you some evening. Would you like to come to my house? I can cook."

His face visibly relaxed at her acceptance, and he actually smiled, showing slightly uneven teeth—just enough to show character. "Maybe some other time. But I was thinking we could go out somewhere, that is, if I can find someone to spend that time with my sister."

Denise couldn't believe what he was saying. On the one hand, she was thrilled to be asked out by this guy, but on the other hand, he wanted someone to sit with his adult sister. "Amy is twenty-three years old."

He shrugged as if he knew he was stepping over the bounds, but couldn't help himself. "I know, and if we were back in Nashville, I wouldn't mind leaving her alone. But she doesn't know anyone here, and she might get lonely."

Denise inhaled deeply. Her work was cut out for her, now that she knew what she was dealing with. As much as she'd vowed to mind her own business, this was one time she simply couldn't. These two people needed her, and she was going to come through for them with flying colors. Andrew obviously didn't know how to help his sister gain independence.

"I'm sure we can find someone to spend that time with her. There are plenty of nice people in Clear-view." Denise figured she'd have to start slowly and work up to getting Amy to stand on her own two feet. It would happen, she was sure, but not immediately.

Andrew grinned. "Good. I'll call you at the store."

Denise also remembered Bethany telling her that she and David were having them all over for dinner on Friday night, but she didn't say anything about it, just in case Andrew didn't know about it yet. Maybe if she and Andrew went out before that, things wouldn't be so awkward at the Hadaways' house.

Things were definitely looking up in Clearview. It was amazing what had happened over the years. Denise couldn't have imagined life without her family, but once her parents had died, she found herself rising to the level of being self-sufficient. But it hadn't come without resistance.

In the beginning, she'd tried living life on the wild side. Although there were some fun moments, it didn't work for her. She was always left the next day with a few memories and even more regrets.

If David hadn't come along when he had, Denise didn't know where she'd be right now, and she might still be searching to find herself. David had only been in the real estate office a few minutes when he had seen her pain through the rough exterior she tried to show the world, and after getting to know her a little better as a friend, he'd helped her see how miserable she was.

At first, she'd balked, but when she saw how peaceful and contented he was, in spite of some of the bad hands he'd been dealt, she realized she could experience the very same thing. So she'd cleaned up her act, gone to work for him at the church, and with his blessing, taken advantage of the town's need for a full-service bookstore. David had even helped her get into her very own house. Her self-respect had returned. Now she was a responsible business owner in her hometown, something that had initially shocked some of the people she'd known all her life.

Gertie Chalmers, Bethany's grandmother, had always kept a close eye on Denise, scrutinizing her every move. But Denise never felt as if Gertie was trying to hurt her. And Gertie was the first person who patted her on the back and told her how proud of her she was. That meant a lot to Denise. Now, Gertie Chalmers was one of Denise's favorite people in the whole wide world.

What she would do for Amy Mitchell was nothing compared to what people had done for her. But it was payback time, and she'd do the best she could.

Denise felt like she had a renewed purpose in life, now that she'd decided to take Amy under her wing. And the fact that Andrew had expressed an interest in her made it even sweeter. Hopefully, things would work out great and they'd have a wonderful time. She didn't want to think beyond that, but she could at least revel in her current thoughts and feelings.

Getting up each morning and going into the bookstore had never been a problem for Denise. She loved everything about owning the place. And now that she had Amy working for her, she looked forward to it even more.

Amy was waiting outside the store when she arrived. “Looks like I might want to get you a key to the place,” Denise said with a sideways smile.

Amy’s eyes widened. “You’d do that? You’d really give me a key?”

“Of course,” Denise answered. “What if I’m running late and I need you to open the store for me?”

Amy hunkered down inside her jacket, her hands in her pockets, a satisfied smile on her lips as she waited for Denise to unbolt the door. Denise could tell she was pleased with that one little vote of confidence she’d just given her new employee. Amy Mitchell was so easy to please, Denise figured she’d have to warn her about a few things.

“We need to work up a schedule for you, Amy,” Denise said as she hung her coat on the rack in the back of the store. “How many hours would you like to have?”

Amy pursed her lips and thought for a moment. Denise could tell she wasn’t used to having to make many decisions on her own. But she would now. Denise could wait all day for an answer if she had to.

Finally, Amy spoke. “Do you mind if I call my brother and ask him?”

Denise started to tell her to go ahead, but then she thought about it. “I don’t want you to do that, Amy.

I want you to tell me how many hours *you* want to work."

The pained expression on Amy's face broke Denise's heart. This woman had been seriously repressed in her life, although she suspected it wasn't done maliciously. Her well-meaning parents had held her social and business development back to the point of making her very unsure of herself. Overprotectiveness had a tendency to do that to a person.

Finally, Amy shrugged and said, "How many hours do you need me?"

That was a reasonable question, Denise thought, although she would have preferred Amy give her more specific times. "I could use you during high-traffic times, like on Saturday mornings and late afternoons. And if you'd like, you can take over the children's story hour. You're pretty good with little people."

Amy's eyes brightened at the compliment. Denise made a mental note to compliment her new employee every chance she got.

It took them most of the morning, between customers, to get the next week's schedule worked out, but they finally did it. "We'll see how it goes, then we can adjust as needed."

Denise and Amy quickly fell into a comfortable pattern of working together. Although Amy wasn't quite ready to be alone in the store yet, Denise figured that would be her next goal—to get Amy confident enough to run the cash register when she was by herself.

Late in the afternoon, Andrew called the store. Denise answered the phone, and she started to hand it to Amy. "No," he said. "I want to talk to you."

Denise's heart sang. "Okay," she said breathlessly. Clearing her throat, she went on. "What can I do for you?"

"I told you I'd call about going out to dinner soon. How's tonight?" His voice sounded a little deeper than usual. Denise felt her hands start to shake.

"That would be nice."

"Have you found someone to spend time with my sister?"

Denise was instantly jerked back to reality. This date with Andrew wasn't only for her pleasure. It was part of her mission to help Amy. "No, not yet. But if you give me a little time, I think I can come up with something for her to do."

"Call me back at the house. I'm working on some accounts here in the study, so I'll be right by the phone."

Denise told Amy that she'd have to use the phone in the back room and to let her know if she was needed. Then, she went straight back to her office and called Bethany. She told her childhood best friend everything that was going on. "Can you hang out with Amy while I go out with Andrew?" Denise begged.

Bethany hesitated for a moment. "No, I'm sorry, Denise, but tonight, we have some people from the church coming over to plan for expansion." Since David had been at New Hope, the place had grown exponentially.

"What can I do?" Denise asked.

"You really want to go out with Andrew, don't you?" Bethany asked. Denise could almost hear her smiling.

"Yes," Denise said, trying hard to cover for the fact that she was embarrassed. "You know I do. When was the last time I turned down a date with someone who looked like that?"

Bethany let out a throaty chuckle. "I can't seem to remember a time you *ever* turned down a date with *anyone*."

Denise started to defend her honor, but she thought better of it. She wanted something from Bethany. "What can I do?"

"Have you called Nana?" Bethany asked, referring to her grandmother. "I'm sure she'd enjoy having company."

"Know what, Bethany?" Denise asked with excitement. "You're brilliant. Gertie Chalmers is just the person to help pull Amy out of her shell."

Bethany sighed. "You're probably right, but there's no telling what Andrew will say once Nana gets through filling her head with all sorts of ideas."

"I know," Denise said, giggling. "And this will be so much fun."

"You always did enjoy getting reactions from people."

Denise swallowed hard and forced the grin from her face. "Well, this is one reaction I'd like to have a picture of."

"Me, too," Bethany said before they hung up.

Gertie was thrilled to hear from Denise. "You know I'd love to entertain a young person, Denise. If she's a friend of yours, she's got to be fun."

"Actually, she's very quiet," Denise said. "I'm hoping you'll help her get over her feelings of inadequacy."

"Oh, this is one of those types of visits, is it?" Gertie said, cackling. "Bring her over. I'll do what I can."

"Thanks so much, Gertie." Denise had been corrected a couple years ago when she'd called Bethany's grandmother Mrs. Chalmers.

"Gertie," the woman had corrected. "You're a grown-up now, Denise. When you call me Mrs. Chalmers, it makes me feel old."

Denise chuckled. Gertie Chalmers was anything but old. That woman constantly defied her age in years by thinking like a very young woman. And she used her rights that came with age by speaking what was on her mind. It was the best of both worlds for her.

"I'll bring her over after work. We'll probably stop somewhere and get a bite to eat," Denise said.

"If you're going to the Burger Barn, would you mind bringing me a chili cheese dog?" Gertie asked, her voice sounding almost like that of a little girl.

Denise chuckled. "Sure, I'll be glad to. Extra onions?"

"Of course."

Denise came out of the back room, feeling like singing. But she didn't. Instead, she headed straight for the shelf where Amy was looking over a selection for someone who stood off to one side.

"When you're finished with this customer, I've got something to tell you," Denise whispered.

Amy nodded, her forehead still crinkled as she was deep in thought. She took her job very seriously, and Denise was very proud of her.

As soon as the customer left the store with a sack full of purchases, Amy turned to Denise. "What did you want to tell me?"

"You have a treat in store for you tonight." Denise could hardly keep the excitement from her voice.

"A treat?" Amy's eyebrows shot up in anticipation.

Denise nodded. "Gertie Chalmers wants to meet you. She's Bethany Hadaway's grandmother."

Amy took a step back. "Why would Bethany's grandmother want to meet me?"

Denise had to think fast on this one. She didn't want it to sound like what it really was—a way to keep Amy from being alone. "Gertie Chalmers is one of those people who wants to meet everyone who's new in town. She's one of the coolest women I've ever known."

With a worried frown, Amy tilted her head to one side. "I still don't know why she'd want to meet me. What about Andrew?"

Amy was much sharper than Denise realized. How would she get out of this one gracefully? she wondered.

"Gertie wants to meet him, too. I thought that maybe he could meet us here after we closed the shop, and we'd ride over there together."

That seemed to satisfy Amy. She nodded. "I guess that would be okay. That is, if Andrew doesn't mind."

"Let me go call him," Denise said. "You're doing such a good job with the customers, I don't mind leaving you alone up here."

Nothing else she could have said would have brought the smile that was now on Amy's face. Denise let out a sigh of relief as she thought about how close she'd come to insulting Amy.

Andrew was reluctant to agree to the terms his sister had unknowingly set up for him. "I don't see why I have to meet her."

"I wasn't kidding when I told Amy that Gertie likes to meet all the new people in town. Besides, you'll like her."

"Okay," he finally agreed. "I suppose that would be okay, considering she's the preacher's wife's grandmother."

What that had to do with anything, Denise didn't know. But she accepted it. Now, she needed to figure out how to leave Amy with Gertie without raising suspicion. She didn't want Amy to think they were treating her like a child, even though they were.

Chapter Five

When Denise returned to the front of the store, Amy had a line of customers. They all seemed to be doing just fine, so Denise let Amy ring up their sales while she helped one of the teenagers who'd come in for something his teacher told him to get.

Within fifteen minutes the store was cleared out, leaving Denise and Amy alone. Amy had a huge smile plastered across her face.

"You look pretty pleased with yourself." Denise leaned against the counter and studied Amy.

"I am," Amy said with a satisfied smile. "I finally feel like I'm contributing something to the world."

"Yes, you are, Amy, and you're doing a fine job of it, too. I like the fact that you're available the hours I need you. Most of my employees give me very strict times they *can't* work, so I have to consider that before I schedule them."

Amy ran her hand gently over the counter and then looked at Denise. "Once Andrew starts going to the office every day, I'd be lonely if I had to stay home all the time. It's nice having a place to go."

"I've got a question for you, Amy," Denise said slowly, not sure if she should go there. But she wasn't one to leave questions unasked. "Do you ever plan to drive?"

Amy shrugged. "I have before. When I was a teenager I had my learner's permit, but my dad decided I was better off with a chauffeur."

"A chauffeur?" Denise squeaked. It was even worse than she'd thought. "We don't have many of those here in Clearview."

"I know," Amy said, nodding. "But I was thinking I'd call a driving school and hire an instructor soon."

Denise burst into a fit of laughter. Amy stared at her in horror. Finally, Denise settled down and gently placed her hand on Amy's shoulder. "The only driving school we have here is in the high school. The instructor is a football coach. Everyone in Clearview learned how to drive with him in the passenger seat."

Amy's face contorted in worry. "Then how will I learn how to drive? There are no chauffeurs here, no reliable public transportation to speak of, and the taxi service doesn't even run half the time."

"Tell you what, Amy," Denise said. "I'll give the

coach a call and see if he has Saturdays free. Maybe he'll be interested in moonlighting."

Amy smiled and let out a sigh of relief. "I would really appreciate it."

"I'll have to warn you, though, Coach Simmons is a crusty old man. He comes across as being pretty crude, but he has a heart of gold."

"Crude?" Amy asked in a fearful voice.

"Yeah, but don't worry. He doesn't mean half of what he says."

"Oh," Amy replied as she backed away from Denise.

Denise hated feeling like she had to shock Amy all the time, but she'd always been blunt. She didn't know any other way to get information across. And the sooner Amy realized how things were in Clearview, the better off she'd be.

"Uh, Denise," Amy said, "Andrew's outside waiting for us. Are you ready to close yet?"

That comment quickly jerked Denise back to what was going on for the moment. She needed to concentrate on more than one thing at a time now, and she was having trouble with it. "Sure. Let me put the money in the bag so we can drop it in the bank night deposit."

Amy actually helped her this time, cutting the amount of time it took in half. "Ready?" Denise said. "Why don't you ride with me, and Andrew can follow us to Gertie's apartment?"

They joined Andrew outside. Amy gave Andrew a big bear hug, touching the tender spot in Denise's heart. She'd often wished for a brother or sister to be close to, but many of her friends had told her that wasn't always the case. In fact, more times than not, they wanted to strangle their siblings.

After making arrangements for Andrew to follow them, Denise and Amy took the lead. They dropped off the deposit, then headed for the retirement center.

Gertie was standing at the door waiting for them. "I baked," she said with excitement.

Denise's mouth watered as she remembered all the treats Gertie had baked for her and Bethany when they were children. Even when Gertie was busy scolding them for something, she was feeding them milk and cookies.

Andrew glanced at Denise and back at Gertie in confusion. Before he had a chance to say something about Amy needing someone to spend time with her so she wouldn't be alone, Denise stepped up and said, "Sounds good, Gertie." She quickly kissed the elderly woman on the cheek.

Gertie clucked as the three younger people followed her to the kitchen table. "Isn't this place great?" she asked. "I can get from one end of the apartment to the other in a matter of seconds. And when I have company I don't have to holler for people to come to the table. They're already there."

Denise admired her spirit, thinking she wanted to

be like that when she was Gertie's age. A good attitude was important as people aged.

Andrew shifted in his chair, obviously trying to figure out how he and Denise would be able to leave without upsetting Amy. Denise didn't know how it would happen, but she knew that Gertie would save the evening for them.

After she placed the warm platter of cookies on the table, Gertie turned to Amy and said, "You're such a pretty girl, Amy."

Amy blushed. "Why thank you, Mrs. Chalmers."

"And brainy, too," Gertie added.

Andrew chuckled. "How would you know that?"

"Anyone who works in a bookstore has to be smart, that's how," Gertie snapped. Denise could tell her friend's grandmother wasn't finished with what she had to say, so she sat and waited for the bomb. Her timing was perfect, too. Gertie slowly turned to Amy, leaned toward her, and said, "Please call me Gertie. Mrs. Chalmers makes me sound so old."

Amy nodded. "Okay, G-Gertie," she stuttered as if she had a hard time getting the first name out.

Gertie turned to Andrew and scowled. "And that goes for you, too, young man."

His eyes grew huge, and he cast a nervous glance over at Denise. "Yes, ma'am."

"Gertie," she said, leveling her gaze on his.

Denise watched as he gulped. "Gertie," he repeated after her.

"Good," Gertie said with a smile of satisfaction. "Now it's time to get down to business. Anyone up for a game of chess?"

With a chuckle, Denise said, "Only two people can play chess, Gertie. Besides, you know I never quite mastered the game."

"Yes, I remember, Denise. I'll bet Amy here can play." All eyes turned to Amy.

With the biggest smile Denise had ever seen on Amy's face, the young woman nodded. "Why, yes, I do play chess. In fact, I was the only girl on the high school chess team."

Denise squinted at Gertie. She must have known that. Somehow.

Gertie whipped out her chess board and motioned for Denise and Andrew to leave her and Amy alone. "You two, run along. I can't concentrate with an audience. Besides, I've got my taste buds set for a good, old fashioned chili cheese dog. Extra onions."

What a sly rascal, Denise thought as she and Andrew got into his car. He drove back toward town a few minutes before he said anything. Finally, when he spoke, his words were filled with reverence toward Gertie.

"How did she do that?" he asked, his voice catching on the words.

"I don't know, but she's good, isn't she?"

"The best," he replied. "I thought my mother was a

champion manipulator, but I think I've just met the one person who could unseat her."

"No doubt," Denise said with a chuckle.

"I thought we might have a steak tonight, but now I'm not sure."

"Maybe we can do that some other time. I wouldn't want to face Gertie without her order. I've been on her bad side before, and trust me, it's not a bit of fun."

They pulled into the Burger Barn parking lot that was nearly empty. "Weeknights aren't their busy time, obviously," Andrew said.

"No, but you should see it on a Friday or Saturday."

"I have."

They went inside and placed their order at the window. The fresh-faced kid behind the counter told them to have a seat and he'd bring their food when it was ready.

Once they were seated, Denise wasn't sure what to talk about. She and Andrew were from two completely different places, although they'd both grown up in the midst of almost obscene wealth. However, it appeared his parents handled it quite differently from hers.

"Have you lived here all your life?" Andrew asked, breaking the silence.

"All my life," Denise replied. "I can't imagine living anywhere else."

"I always thought the same thing about Nashville, but when this opportunity with Swetson's came up, I couldn't pass it up."

"How did you even know about it?" Denise had been curious, but this was the first time she had the opportunity to ask. She wasn't about to let it go.

"One of my dad's friends is a stockholder of the company. They've been expanding rapidly, which is why they moved here to Clearview."

She should have known. Andrew got his job through connections. Somehow, she felt let down. But she couldn't tell him that.

"So, do you like it?" Denise asked to change the subject.

"Like what?" he asked. "Burger Barn?"

She laughed. "No, Clearview."

"Oh, Clearview," Andrew said, leaning back and taking a long look around the fast food restaurant dining room. "It seems like a very pleasant place to live."

"You picked a nice neighborhood." The instant Denise said that, she felt like she'd stuck her foot in her mouth.

He let out a sigh. "I never would have picked a place like Allendale if I'd had my say. And I certainly wouldn't have bought that monstrosity of a house."

"Really? What's wrong with it?"

"It's too big, too gaudy, and too dark."

Denise agreed, but she didn't want to be rude. "I offered to help Amy decorate it."

"That should keep her out of trouble for a while." His tone sounded like that of a stressed parent.

"Trouble?" Denise said, her voice coming out almost in a shriek. "Amy isn't a bit of trouble. In fact, I find her quite the opposite."

Andrew closed his eyes, breathed deeply, then opened them again. "Denise, I'm really sorry, but I seem to keep saying the wrong things around you. I love my sister, but in case you haven't noticed, she's not exactly the most mature person in the world. I worry about her."

"Then let her go." There. She'd said it, and she couldn't take it back.

"Let her go?" Andrew glared at her.

"Yes, let her go. I'm not talking about abandoning her. She's your sister, and you can't do that. What I'm talking about is giving her credit for having a little sense."

"But what if she makes a mistake? My parents would be terribly disappointed."

Denise shook her head. "Trust me, she *will* make a mistake. And it might even be a doozy. She might even make a bunch of mistakes. But that's the only way she'll learn that she's a capable person."

Andrew laughed. "Capable? Somehow I don't think that would be enough for my dad. He wants me to continue his job of being her father since she's in my care now. I'm just an extension of our parents."

"Then be a good parent to her and give her some rope, a little at a time."

"Has anyone ever told you to mind your own business?" Andrew asked.

"Of course," Denise said, trying hard not to feel offended. Other people had told her many times to keep her nose to herself, but this time it felt different. "Is that what you're saying?"

Andrew hesitated for a moment and did the total opposite of what Denise expected. "No, I'm not saying that. I might need to ask your advice, and I wouldn't want to alienate you." His voice sounded tired, the very reason Denise couldn't be angry with him. He really did care about his sister.

At that very moment, Denise felt like a tight bond had formed between them. It felt wonderful to be in on something with this man.

"I'll do what I can, Andrew. Amy's a very sweet girl."

Andrew smiled warmly at Denise. It felt so right to her for the two of them to be sitting across the table from each other. It didn't matter where they were. They could be anywhere—Burger Barn or the fanciest restaurant in town.

Denise sure did look wonderful tonight, Andrew thought. He'd thought she was attractive before, when they'd first met, but now, after spending time with her and getting to know her, she was downright gorgeous.

The fact that she took a special interest in his baby sister didn't hurt, either. From the moment Amy was brought home, Andrew felt protective of her, even more than most big brothers felt, he suspected. She seemed so fragile, so lost, so totally unsure of everything around her, he wanted to always be there for her. But he knew he couldn't. There were times when she needed space from him. And right now, he was enjoying not worrying about her.

In spite of Gertie Chalmers's crustiness, he knew she was trustworthy. She was also very crafty, so he had to keep an eye on her. Otherwise, she'd fill his little sister with all sorts of ideas, some of them probably not ones he'd want her to have.

He chuckled at the thought of what his mom and dad would do if they knew he'd left Amy in the care of an old woman in a retirement center. Her apartment was smaller than the foyer of the house he shared with Amy.

"Whatcha thinkin' about?" Denise said, startling him from his thoughts.

Andrew glanced up from beneath hooded eyes. "Do you think Amy will be all right with Gertie?"

"Of course," Denise said with a smirk. "Exactly what can go wrong with a little old lady and a young, female chess champion?"

He let out a sigh. "You're right. It's just that I'm so used to having to think of her first, I have a hard time concentrating on anything else."

The instant he said that, he knew it was a lie. He'd thought about how much fun he was having with Denise and how he'd like to be with her again. He hadn't thought much of Amy since he'd been with Denise.

That should have annoyed him rather than brought him pleasure. First things first, and right now he needed to concentrate on his new job and his sister.

Besides, Andrew could picture that mischievous look on Gertie's face. That woman, as innocent as she tried to make herself look and sound, could really pull a fast one if she went unchecked.

"Should we call Gertie?" he asked. "The food's not here yet."

Denise's eyebrows shot up, then a grin split her face. "You've got to be kidding. That would be an insult to both Gertie and Amy. Can't you leave them alone for a few hours without worrying? They're two grown women who can enjoy each other's company if we let them."

Andrew glanced down at the table, then back up at Denise. Was she mocking him? No, her eyes didn't hold that kind of expression. What was that he saw on her face? Was it pity? No, that wasn't it, either.

He finally let out the breath he'd been holding. "I guess I need to learn to let go."

"That's what I keep trying to tell you, Andrew," Denise said as the fresh-faced kid brought two trays filled with food.

It was Andrew's turn to raise his eyebrows. "I can't believe we ordered so much."

Denise chuckled. "It always looks like more than it is because they wrap every single thing in paper. It's kind of like presents under the Christmas tree. When they're wrapped they seem much more special than they would be if they came exposed."

Andrew had never heard of fast food being compared to presents beneath a tree, but he liked the analogy. Nodding, he replied, "You've got a good point there."

"I generally do," Denise said as she sank her teeth into her hamburger. She shoved a packet of onion rings toward Andrew. "Here. Try one of these. They really know how to fry onions here."

Andrew had more fun with Denise than he'd ever had with the debutantes he'd dated in Nashville. She had class, but she wasn't stuffy. She was fun-loving and filled with all sorts of surprises, totally the opposite of the women he'd known before. She was also the most self-sufficient woman he'd ever met.

After they finished eating, Denise's mouth widened in a satisfied smile. "Wasn't that wonderful?"

"Yes," Andrew said, nodding. "I have to admit, I've never had anything quite like it."

"You didn't answer my question," Denise said as her smile faded. "Did you like it?" she repeated.

He nodded. "Yes, very much." What Andrew had liked most was the company he was keeping. Denise's anecdotes had kept him in stitches, and she'd brought brightness to his day that was otherwise filled with dull numbers and the inside of that old house his father had bought for Amy.

Denise grabbed her purse and stood up. "We need to order something for Gertie and Amy."

"I don't know about Amy." Somehow, Andrew couldn't imagine his very prim and proper little sister eating something from the Burger Barn.

"Oh, don't be such a stick-in-the-mud, Andrew. Let Amy be the judge of this fine cuisine. I bet she'll love it." She'd already turned and headed for the order counter, leaving him standing there with his hands in his pockets.

By the time Andrew joined Denise, she'd already ordered two chili cheese dogs, extra onions, and a couple large orders of fries. "And throw in two chocolate malteds while you're at it, Derek," she told the boy. She turned to Andrew. "Derek's mom used to babysit me when she was his age. Man, did we have fun!"

Andrew chuckled. "What did you do?"

"We ordered food from everyone in town who delivered, and we played all the teenage music she brought over. She even taught me how to dance."

Denise was filled with more enthusiasm than Andrew had ever seen in a roomful of people before. She seemed to find fun in everything she did. This touched his heart and made him realize how much his life was lacking in the laughter department.

All the way back to Gertie's apartment, Denise chattered incessantly. It was hard for Andrew to keep up with all she told him, but he tried. Unlike some of the other women he'd known, she was interesting. She understood sports, she loved to eat, and she had so many friends he doubted he'd be able to keep track of them all. Besides all that, she was entrepreneurial. Her business seemed to be thriving, something he knew was difficult to do these days.

Andrew helped Denise carry the food to Gertie's door. It opened before they had a chance to knock.

"I thought you'd never get here. Amy and I are about to starve to death." Her raspy voice sounded cute to Andrew.

The table had been cleared, and Amy was still sitting there with a cup of tea in front of her. Andrew glanced at her and tilted his head, as if to ask her if she was okay. She smiled back at him contentedly.

"Gertie and I were just sitting here having an old-fashioned chat."

Waving her hand around, Gertie said, "Men don't care about those things, Amy. At least they never did in my day." She turned to Denise. "What took you so long to get back?"

"We ate there, Gertie. I thought you knew we were going to do that."

"Yes, of course I did. But you didn't have to take all night." Her words belied her good-natured manner. Denise reached over and hugged the woman she'd had to win over as a friend. Andrew was amazed at all the things Denise had told him, one of which was how Gertie tried to keep Bethany and Denise apart because of how much trouble they seemed to get into when they were together.

Andrew watched as they unfolded paper and pulled food from the wrappers. Amy reached for her plate as if she hadn't eaten in years. The aroma of the food wafted through the tiny apartment, and he found himself looking around at the furnishings. Gertie had quite a few nice things crammed into the small space. He could tell she held some of her belongings near and dear to her heart.

"Mmm," his sister said, "This is yummy."

Andrew flinched. "You like that?"

Amy's eyes lit up as they looked at each other. "I love it."

If his parents knew he'd brought his sister carry-out food from the Burger Barn, they'd skin him alive. But it was time she started to live a normal life, so he'd have to turn his back to give her some space.

"Gertie seems to think I'd look better if I wore my hair differently," Amy said. "What do you think?"

"No!" Andrew said before he knew who she was talking to. His mother had helped her coax her wavy hair into the long strands she put in a twist on top of her head. It had taken forever, and he didn't want to tamper with something so important.

Denise shot him a dirty look. "I think you'd look cute with a more modern cut, Amy. Why don't you let me take you to the Cut 'n Curl next week? Connie can work wonders with curly hair."

Gertie glanced back and forth between Andrew and Denise before she said, "Maybe you'd better wait a while on that, Denise. Let Amy get used to living in Clearview first. This must be a big adjustment for her, and we don't want to overload her."

"No!" Amy said, her jaw firmly set. "I want to go to the Cut 'n Curl next week. A new hair style would be fun. I'm sick and tired of having to put my hair up every single day."

Andrew felt defeated. What would his parents say when he brought home a different person than what he'd left with? But he couldn't argue with these people right now. He'd have to discuss this with Amy when they were alone.

Denise narrowed her focus on him. He couldn't help but notice that her friendly expression had been replaced by something else—something that looked an awful lot like anger.

Chapter Six

Denise had never felt so helpless in all her life. Here she was with these romantic feelings for some guy who had a paternal urge toward his full-grown sister. She wanted to reach out, yank him up by his perfectly starched collar, and give him a piece of her mind.

But Gertie was right. They had plenty of time to make changes. The Cut 'n Curl wasn't going anywhere. And Amy still had quite a few things she needed to learn. If she tried to do too much, it might push her right over the edge, not to mention what it would do to her brother and parents.

Denise reached out and touched Amy's arm. "I'll help you figure something else out to do with your hair, but Gertie has a good point. You don't want to make too many changes too fast. Besides, I still need to call Coach Simmons."

"Coach Simmons?" Andrew asked, looking suspiciously at Amy.

His sister nodded in defiance. "The driving instructor."

"Driving instructor?" he repeated.

Denise actually felt sorry for Andrew. Here he was being slammed with all sorts of things his sister wanted to do, and he obviously felt helpless about all of it.

"He's the only person in Clearview who's certified to teach driving," Denise explained.

Andrew shook his head. "I can take her wherever she needs to go."

"No, you can't," Amy said as she stood up beside her brother. "I want to learn to drive and get my own car. I want freedom."

Whoa! thought Denise. Now she knew he'd go ballistic. She had to do something, and she had to do it fast.

"Uh, Amy, honey," Denise said as she tugged on Amy's arm, "why don't you slow down a bit? We can take these changes one at a time. There's no hurry."

Amy opened her mouth, but she didn't say a word. As she clamped her jaw shut, she nodded and sat back down.

Gertie had remained quieter than usual through all

this, which surprised Denise. Usually Gertie had a lot to say about everything.

Denise decided to change the subject. "Bethany told me she wants all of us at her house on Friday night. That's something I wouldn't want to miss for the world."

"Yes, she did tell me she wanted me to come early to help her bake," Gertie said, taking the hint and joining in the new topic of discussion.

"In that case," Denise said with enthusiasm, "no one wants to miss the dinner party. Gertie bakes the best pastries in Clearview."

Andrew let out a deep sigh as he nodded. "Amy and I are looking forward to it."

Amy glared at him. "Let me talk for myself." Then she turned and smiled at Gertie and Denise. "I'm really looking forward to Friday night."

Denise froze in her position. Only her eyes moved. As she looked at Gertie, she saw a smile threatening to break through in the older woman's face. But it didn't. Gertie somehow managed to use self-restraint, something she generally didn't bother with.

"Well, good," Gertie finally said. "We'll have fun. I might even challenge you to a rematch."

Amy chuckled. "I don't know why you'd do that. You beat me."

Andrew's head jerked around. "You beat my sister?" he said in astonishment.

Gertie nodded and winked. "That was just the first game. I'll bet next time she beats my socks off."

With obvious delight, Amy giggled. "I doubt it. Gertie's good."

Denise studied Andrew's reaction. He was clearly surprised and impressed at the fact that Gertie had won a chess match with his sister. She had a feeling he'd be surprised at a lot of things as he spent more time in Clearview. This appeared to be a sleepy little town with laidback citizens, but beneath the surface there was a lot going on.

After Andrew and Amy left, Denise turned to Gertie and said, "Well, what do you think?"

Gertie did her best to stifle her smile, leaving a goofy expression and a smirk. "What do I think of what?"

Denise rolled her eyes. "You know. The Mitchells."

"They're a very nice pair of young people."

Groaning, Denise plopped down in the rocking chair Bethany's husband had made from the oak tree he'd had to cut down from the backyard of what used to be Gertie's house. "Do you think Amy will ever be liberated from that overbearing brother of hers?"

"He's not overbearing," Gertie argued, avoiding answering Denise's question.

"Not overbearing?" Denise shrieked. "What do you call a brother when he tells his grown sister she can't change her hair, she can't drive, and she has to have someone sit with her when he goes somewhere without her?"

Now, Gertie smiled. In fact, she laughed out loud. "I call that a very caring, doting brother who is clueless about what he's supposed to do with his sister."

"He can leave her alone and let her make her own decisions, that's what he can do," Denise roared.

"It's not that easy." Gertie stood there with her finger on her chin. "Remember when I had my stroke last year?"

Denise nodded. "How could I forget?"

"I kept hearing people around me talking about what they were going to do with me. They seemed to think I didn't know what was going on, but I did. Sure, I had temporary lapses of memory, but my hearing was great. And I could actually feel myself getting better every day. My headaches started out being horrendous, but they subsided. And I was able to walk with assistance after a couple weeks. But those people still kept talking about me like I was a child."

"Didn't that make you mad?" Denise asked. She knew Gertie was going somewhere with this, and she was curious.

"Not really," Gertie replied as she sat on the loveseat across from the rocking chair. "It actually made me feel good."

"It did?"

"Yes. Their concern showed me that they cared. The only person I was worried about was Bethany, but it didn't take me long to figure out that David was the perfect match for her."

Denise chuckled. "I saw that, too. Too bad it took them so long to see it."

"Things generally happen in their own time if we allow it."

Gertie was such a wise woman, Denise never dreamed of arguing with her. Almost everything the older woman said, even when it wasn't obvious at the time, turned out to be right on the money.

"Well, I'd better get a move on," Denise said as she stood up. "I'm still training Amy, so I can't leave her alone in the store yet."

"She's almost ready," Gertie said. "Don't wait too long before you give her full responsibility."

Denise opened her mouth to argue, but she thought better of it. Gertie was right. And she didn't need to treat the bookstore like it was a baby.

Now that her first semi-date with Andrew was behind her, Denise felt like she should be able to relax now. But she knew she couldn't. Those couple of hours spent alone with him made her even more tense. She felt like she was a teenager all over again, wanting to make a good impression on the new guy in town, yet feeling loyalty to Amy, who needed her help.

In spite of her racing mind, sleep came quickly for Denise. But she dreamed a bunch of wild, vivid dreams, many of them set in her childhood home.

The house her parents had bought was just a couple

streets over from Amy's and Andrew's. Her mother had taken one look around and said it was perfect; however, she needed to make a few changes. And those changes were drastic, too, from what Denise remembered. All the flocked wallpaper was stripped, and the dark paint was replaced with brighter colors. That alone made a huge difference. But what she'd done with the kitchen and the sitting room had made the house seem more like a home than a mausoleum.

The kitchen was wallpapered with a bright floral print with a white background. And all the fabric accents picked up the yellows and bright greens from the print.

The sitting room was decorated like a French country garden with flowers everywhere. She'd put out bowls of silk flowers, dried flowers, and whenever they were available, fresh-cut flowers. The place was so cheerful, no one could frown once they entered the room.

When Denise awoke, she knew what she was going to do. So many changes needed to take place in Amy's life, but Denise decided to start with the house. At least, that wouldn't upset Andrew so much, she thought. He'd even said he didn't like the place.

As usual, Amy was waiting outside the store for her when she arrived. "I'll run out and get a key made for you this afternoon, Amy. I want you to start opening the store a couple days a week, starting next week."

Amy's eyes widened. "Are you sure?"

"I'm positive," Denise answered quickly. She didn't want to think too much about it, or she might change her mind. Gertie was right. Amy was perfectly capable of handling things alone, even now. She'd already learned how to operate the cash register, and she was wonderful with customers. Children loved her, and so did the elderly citizens of Clearview. It was almost like a match made in heaven—Amy, Denise, and Carson's Bookstore.

"I'm going to teach you to catalog shipments when they arrive," Denise said as she cut open the box that had been delivered the day before. "We enter all the books in the computer by name, author, subject, and quantity, so when we ring up the sale, we know what we have left."

Amy nodded. She'd already been shown how to check if they had a certain book on the shelf, so she knew about the computer system. "How often do you get shipments in?"

Denise grinned impishly. "As often as we order them."

They both laughed. Denise loved the comfortable way she and Amy had fallen into a pattern of understanding each other. And she had to admit, she loved hearing about Amy's brother, which she did often.

Amy was obviously proud of Andrew and all his accomplishments. Denise learned that he'd graduated valedictorian of his high school class, and then he went on to college, walking away with top honors there.

"Did he ever have a serious girlfriend?" Denise asked, wishing she hadn't the instant the words came out.

"No, not really," Amy replied. "He dated a lot of girls, but none of them seemed to hold his interest for very long. Andrew's a peculiar sort of guy. He's the type of man who'll expect his feminine companion to keep up with him on all levels—intelligence, social, and physical. Oh, did I tell you he runs marathons?"

"No," Denise said with a laugh. "But I'm not surprised. He does everything, so why shouldn't he run?"

Denise didn't like to run, but she managed to stay in shape by walking several miles every day, either in the morning or early evening. She loved parties, and although she didn't make wonderful grades, she knew she was smart. But it was the kind of intelligence that couldn't be measured by test grades. She had common sense, now that she'd survived her teenage years; and she had managed to absorb some book knowledge, at least what she needed for business. On top of all that, she was a voracious reader, with at least half a dozen books on her nightstand at any given time.

"I think he likes you, Denise," Amy said.

Denise's face instantly heated up, so she tried to cover for the embarrassment of the pleasure of Amy's comment. "I like him, too. He seems very nice."

Amy studied her for a moment before she shook her head. "No, I mean I think he *really likes* you."

Denise had to turn her head to keep her employee from seeing the stupid grin that had taken over her face. And she forced herself not to say that she *really liked* Andrew, too.

They worked in silence for the next few minutes, unpacking and stacking the books in alphabetical order by author. When they'd broken down and discarded all the boxes, Denise turned to Amy. "Now the fun really begins."

She worked with Amy, teaching her everything she needed to know about cataloging and shelving books. Amy caught on fast, to Denise's delight, and they were soon finished.

"That was fun!" Amy said as she stood up straight and brushed her hands together.

"We'll see if you're still saying that after the tenth time you have to do this. It can get pretty tedious after a while."

"Oh, but I love everything about working here," Amy said. "I never imagined having a job would be so wonderful."

Denise was pleased with Amy, too, and she'd told her often. She wasn't the type of employer who believed in holding back compliments. One thing that surprised her, though, was the fact that Amy seemed satisfied with her first paycheck. It wasn't much, and Denise knew it. Most of the people who'd worked for her had expressed their displeasure over the paltry amount on the face of the check. Denise would have paid them more if she could, but she couldn't. It was just a small business, and she had no desire to grow beyond that.

When Denise had pointed out that Amy's wages would have been much higher somewhere else, Amy just shook her head. "You don't understand. It's not the money, it's everything else. For the first time in my life I feel like what I do matters."

Denise understood that better than anyone else possibly could. In some ways she and Amy couldn't have been more different. But then in other ways, they were so much alike it was scary. When Amy expressed dismay over something, Denise felt as though she was reliving the days of her late teens and early twenties.

For the rest of the week, Denise taught Amy everything she could think of about the bookstore business. They went over all the lessons more than once, until Amy said, "I'm ready to handle the store alone now, so when you want to take a day off, please do it."

Denise let out a long sigh of relief. "I'm glad you said that, Amy, because I'm in dire need of some time off."

Nodding, Amy agreed. "No one can work the kind of hours you put in and not feel the effects."

It was heartwarming that Amy had noticed. Now that Denise didn't have any living relatives, she often wondered if anyone would notice when she needed something. And she wasn't the type to ask for help.

On Friday afternoon, Amy turned to Denise and said, "Why don't you go home and relax for the rest of the day? I can close up here."

"Are you sure?" Denise asked. She knew Amy was capable of handling things, but she didn't want to rush her.

"I'm positive. I want you to be fresh for the dinner party tonight."

With a light chuckle, Denise said, "Fresh? For what? With David, Bethany, and Gertie in the kitchen, no one else needs to do anything. All three of them are wonderful cooks."

"I want you to be fresh for my brother. I think it would be nice for the two of you to get together." Amy said that in such a matter-of-fact way and with such a soft voice, it was almost as if she was telling her about the weather. Denise almost choked on air from surprise.

"I'll be fine," Denise finally said as she recovered. "But I think I will take your advice and go home early. You know how to run this place single-handedly, and I have no doubt you'll do a great job."

In spite of Denise's confidence in Amy's abilities to run the store, she left a detailed set of instructions. "And don't hesitate to call if you need something."

"Bye," Amy said firmly. "I'll be fine. See you tonight."

All the way home, Denise felt like she'd had a tremendous burden lifted from her shoulders. As much as she loved having her bookstore, she rarely took a break. In the past, she'd had several people who were capable of running the place in her absence, but each of them wound up leaving for various reasons. One of these days, Denise was certain, Amy would leave, too. But at least she had her for now.

Denise decided to lie down for a few minutes before getting ready for the dinner party. She'd already selected the clothes she'd wear—a pair of tweed wool slacks and a cream-colored silk blouse with a V collar. She knew the combination was plain, so she selected some of her larger pieces of jewelry for accent.

After a half-hour rest with her eyes closed, Denise got up and took a fragrant bubble bath. It sure was nice to have this kind of time to get ready, something she hadn't had in what seemed like ages. Thanks to Amy, she'd feel refreshed and relaxed.

She was the first person to arrive besides Gertie. David's nephew Jonathan opened the door before she had a chance to ring the bell. "Hi, Denise!" he shouted as he ran past her and onto the porch. "Where's everyone else?"

Denise shrugged. "I don't know, Jonathan. Some people like to be fashionably late."

"What's fashibly late?" he asked.

"It means that some people like to make an entrance. They don't want to be the first people at a party."

His eyes wide and his expression sincere, Jonathan shook his head. "Oh, this isn't a party, Denise. We're just eating supper."

Denise tousled his hair as she chuckled to herself. Jonathan was such an open and honest kid. She hoped he would never lose that trait, but she was afraid he probably would one of these days.

Gertie was in the kitchen putting the finishing touches on a pie. When she heard Denise enter the room, she smiled. "They put me in charge of desserts, so I'm the one to blame if you go away with an unsatisfied sweet tooth. David and Bethany will be down later."

"What kind of pie are you baking, Gertie?" Denise asked.

"That's a pecan pie. But I just put a lemon meringue pie in the refrigerator. And the chocolate cake over there still needs icing. Jonathan said he wanted gingerbread, so I did those, too."

"You haven't lost your touch, Gertie. You really know the way to my heart." Denise's mouth watered at the suggestion of such a wonderful selection of sweets. "What are David and Bethany cooking?"

"I think they're baking a chicken and a roast. At least that's what it smells like."

Denise crossed the room and opened both doors of the double oven. "Yep, you're right. Chicken and roast beef." She took a step back and added, "And all my favorite vegetables to go with it."

Gertie didn't waste a moment before joining Denise and putting her arm around her. "I know how much you miss your mother, Denise. It hurts a lot."

With a quick sniffle, Denise nodded. "It's nice to have your understanding, Gertie."

"You know you can talk to me any time you feel the need."

"Yes, I know that."

Just then, Jonathan came running back to the kitchen. "Those fashibly late people are here now, Denise."

She was so embarrassed she felt like she wished she had a hole to crawl into. In Jonathan's innocence, he'd blurted out exactly what she'd said earlier.

Hopefully, they didn't hear the little boy. But one look at Andrew and Amy, who trailed behind him, told her they had heard him.

"We're not always late," Andrew said to Jonathan. "But we did feel like we should give Denise a chance to get here first."

Jonathan grinned up at them and added, "And you wanted to make an entrance, too. That's what Denise said."

Chapter Seven

Denise looked at Gertie, who stood there smirking, then back at Andrew and Amy. With a sheepish grin, she said, "And what a nice entrance, too."

Jonathan looked pretty pleased with himself, almost as if he'd made something wonderful happen. Denise had known better than to try to cover anything up because from her experience she knew that would only dig her hole deeper.

"I'm sorry," Andrew said in an even tone. "My sister had some lame notion of trying to do something different with her hair."

Amy's forced smile turned upside down. "I thought it looked good."

Denise let out a sigh of relief. She didn't like Andrew and Amy not getting along, which was obviously the case right now, but at least the focus was off her faux pas.

"Maybe you can show me your new hairstyle later, Amy," Denise said.

Gertie pulled the pie from the oven. "Amy's a pretty girl, Andrew. I don't know why you insist she wear that stodgy hairstyle. It's not appropriate for someone her age. My age, maybe, but not a young girl who should be showing off that beautiful face."

Andrew stepped forward. "Amy doesn't need to show anything off, Gertie." His voice was brusque, like he didn't want to discuss it anymore.

Instead of being put off by him, Gertie just laughed. "Classic older-brother-trying-to-protect-the-younger-sister syndrome."

Denise couldn't look at anyone after that comment, but she would have given her right arm to see their faces. Amy was probably having to hold back a smile, and Andrew was most likely ready to take Gertie's head off. This should be a very interesting dinner party, Denise thought.

"Where are the kids?" Jonathan asked, his voice shrill with excitement.

"You *are* the kid, Jonathan," Gertie said without missing a beat.

He pouted. "But I thought Denise said this was a party."

Gertie chuckled. "I suppose you'd think sitting

around the table with a bunch of grownups would be pretty boring, wouldn't you?"

"It sure would," he replied.

"I just might have something for you in my car, Jonathan," Gertie said without looking at him. "After I finish with these desserts, maybe you can help me fetch it."

His eyes lit up. "I'll help you."

"Now be a good boy and go tell David and Bethany they have company. I don't know what's taking them so long."

Jonathan didn't waste any time. He turned and ran upstairs to get his uncle and aunt because he knew that the sooner everything happened, the sooner he'd get whatever it was Gertie had for him.

With a twinkle in her eye, Gertie announced to the group, "I keep a stash of new toys in my closet so I can bring him a surprise whenever I need one. I even wrap 'em so he'll think they're more special than they are."

Denise grinned at the awesome woman. "That's so sweet, Gertie."

The older woman shook her head. "They're really not expensive or big toys. I just like to make the kid feel special whenever he is disappointed about something. And trust me, that child has had more than his share of disappointments in his life."

Jonathan's parents had been on the brink of divorce for as long as she could remember. That was why he'd spent so much time with David and Bethany. Denise felt for the little boy, and she decided to start bringing children's books with her whenever she visited. Gertie had the right idea.

Andrew and Amy probably didn't understand the dynamics of this family yet, but Denise knew it would be better if she didn't explain too much too soon. They'd find out on their own in due time.

Bethany walked into the kitchen with Emily in her arms. Everyone dropped what they were doing to smile and coo over the baby.

"Is that the baby you had in the store the first day we walked in?" Andrew said as he stared at Emily.

Denise said, "Yes, that's Princess Emily."

He reached toward her. "Do you mind if I hold her? It's been a long time since I've had a baby in my arms."

Bethany didn't hesitate. She gently placed Emily in Andrew's arms.

Andrew and Emily couldn't take their eyes off each other, something that amazed Denise. She remembered how he'd known how to stop her crying, and now she was curious.

Taking a step forward, Denise cleared her throat. Andrew glanced up at her. "How do you know so much about babies?"

Amy groaned. "Now everyone gets to hear the story about how you raised me."

"Well, it's true," Andrew said as he touched Emily's pudgy cheek.

"I know, but you don't like to leave anything out," Amy whined. "Some of it's embarrassing."

Denise chuckled. "Tell us, Andrew. And don't leave anything out."

She didn't dare look at Amy because she knew she'd get one of those frustrated glances Amy often shot at her brother. They were ganging up on her, which was probably good. It would eventually make Amy stand up for herself and take action to be liberated as a grown woman.

Andrew told the story about how he was eight years older than his baby sister and that his parents were often gone. "They always left some of the domestic staff in charge of us, but most of the time we were ignored the second my parents walked out the door. So I took it upon myself to be the one responsible for my baby sister."

Denise felt a tug at her heart. What Andrew just said explained a lot about his and Amy's relationship.

"I took her out in her stroller for long walks," he continued. "I read books to her when she could sit up. I even changed her diapers, one of the awful but necessary jobs of parenting."

Amy groaned. Denise could tell she'd had to listen to his memories before, more than once.

"Go on," Denise prodded, having to hold her side

to keep from laughing. This was getting good—not what Andrew was saying, but Amy's reaction.

Andrew talked for the next ten minutes, telling tale after tale, all the while holding Emily like a fragile piece of china. "And she cried a lot, too," he said. "That's when one of the nannies down the street told me of the football hold. It always worked."

"Football hold?" Bethany said. "Show me."

He carefully demonstrated it with Emily, being very careful not to upset her. She actually seemed to enjoy it.

Denise spoke up. "That's what he told me to do when she wouldn't stop crying in the store. I didn't quite have his technique, but then again I've never held a football before, either."

Everyone laughed. David appeared at the door.

"What's so funny?" he asked, rubbing his chin. Emily began to gurgle, causing him to turn and look at her. "Is my little girl acting up again?"

His voice was filled with pride and joy, something that made Denise's heart do a little twist. She knew that having a baby had brought more joy into Bethany's life than anything else ever had, and she wanted it for herself as well. But how could she have that and what she had—a business *and* her own little house with no one to have to answer to? She knew she couldn't. Well, at least she had something, and she wasn't forced to make a decision.

After everyone took a turn holding Emily, Bethany

carried her back to the nursery. "Don't forget to turn on the baby monitor, Bethany," David called after her. "I'll take care of the one in the kitchen."

Gertie nudged Denise in the side. "Every room in this house is wired so they can hear that baby. I feel sorry for the poor kid when she gets older. She won't get away with a dad-burned thing."

This made everyone laugh. Gertie had a way with words, and she seemed to understand the psyche of a child pretty well, too.

"I thought we'd eat in the dining room, but Gertie thinks it would be cozier to stay in the kitchen," Bethany said. Her eyebrows raised, she asked, "What do you all think?"

Everyone agreed that the kitchen would be better. David had built a long table that would hold as many people as they had without cramping anyone. And they also decided that it would be easier to leave the food in pots on the stove and fill their plates buffet-style.

"With a baby to take care of, I wouldn't want to pile extra work on you," Andrew said.

Denise shot him a wicked glance. "Don't worry about that, Andrew. Around here, the hosts cook the meal, but the guests do the dishes."

Gertie grinned. "If everyone chips in, we can get it done in no time." She was put in charge of seating arrangements, so she placed Andrew across the table from Denise and Amy across from herself. "I want to chat with this delightful girl," she explained.

Amy's face lit up like a light bulb. Andrew looked at Gertie wearily. "Just don't fill her head with too much nonsense."

Denise laughed. "Trust me, Gertie will do exactly that. But don't worry, most of the time no one will get hurt. And if they do, Gertie will take care of them."

Everyone was in a wonderful mood, the conversation was lively, and the food was delicious. "I can't remember ever having so much food at one sitting," Andrew said as he pushed his chair back.

Amy agreed. "And everything was so tasty. I'd like to have the recipes for all of it."

Andrew shook his head. "You'd better learn to boil water first, Amy."

Denise shot a glance in his direction, then slowly turned her head to see Amy's reaction. Fortunately, she wasn't mad. She actually looked amused.

"Mother never allowed me to go in the kitchen when the cook was working," Amy explained. "She was afraid I'd get in the way."

Denise's heart went out to the poor rich young woman who had missed so many of the important things in life that could have brought her so much pleasure. Well, it wasn't too late for her, she thought. She could still experience them.

Gertie was the first one to start clearing the table. "I was thinking that Amy and I could carry the dishes to the sink and get started while Denise and Andrew go for a little walk around the block. Then, when they get back, they can finish up while I show Amy where my garden used to be."

Denise turned to Amy and explained. "This used to be Gertie's house. She sold it to Bethany when she decided to move into the retirement apartment."

"I grew up here," Bethany added.

Andrew hesitated while he seemed to be processing all this new information. Then he turned to Denise and offered an arm. "Shall we take Gertie's suggestion and go for a stroll?"

It sounded so formal to Denise, she let out a quick giggle. He looked serious, so she stifled it. "Sure," she said. "Sounds good."

"Take your time," Gertie hollered as they left the room. "We have plenty to keep us busy for a while."

"Leave us something to do," Denise said with humor. She turned to Andrew and whispered, "Gertie loves hanging out in the kitchen. She's the most domestic person I ever met."

"I can tell," he said. "And it seems to agree with her, too. Do you think she misses this old house?"

"Of course, she does. But at least her granddaughter is living here, so she can come whenever she feels like it."

Andrew was fun to chat with as they wound their way up and down the streets, walking on the sidewalks that were well lit by street lights. "This is such a nice, peaceful town," Andrew commented.

"Yes, it is," Denise agreed. "I've always loved living here."

"I hope Amy and I are able to find our niche." Andrew's voice sounded wistful. Something was bothering him, but Denise didn't want to pry. He was already having to deal with the newness of it all.

"I'm sure you will."

He stopped and turned to look at Denise. "You've never been new to a place where you felt like you were the only outsider, have you?"

"No, not since college," Denise replied. "But I wasn't there long enough to worry about it." She bit her lip and thought for a moment before asking, "Is that how you feel? Like an outsider?"

Andrew resumed walking. He thrust his hands in his pockets as he spoke softly. "Sometimes."

"Do you want to go back?"

"Not really. I like it here. But I have to give myself and Amy some time to adjust to some of the things we've never experienced before."

"Like what, for instance?" Denise asked. It seemed like the right time to start asking questions, since he'd been so open about his feelings.

"Like the fact that no one knows us. In Nashville, everyone knew the Mitchell family. We were treated almost like royalty."

"And you're not here," Denise offered. "But I'd like

to tell you something that might make you feel a little better."

"What's that?"

"No one is treated like royalty around here. Not even the very wealthy."

Andrew chuckled. "I noticed. And that's quite refreshing, in my opinion."

"How does Amy feel?"

"I'm not sure. She seems to be doing just fine. I know she loves working at the bookstore with you." Andrew pulled his hand out of his pocket and took Denise's hand as casually as if it was something he did all the time. "I'd like to thank you for being so nice to her."

"Andrew, you never have to thank me for being nice," Denise said. "People *should* be nice to each other. We should expect it."

That was one of the things Andrew liked about Denise. She was so direct and sincere. And she was probably the nicest person he'd ever met in his life.

He could tell she came from a similar upbringing, but there were some major differences. She seemed more grounded. She seemed more experienced. And she seemed to be the type of person who couldn't be held back from doing whatever she set her mind to do.

Andrew had fought for his independence, but he never would have thought to make waves at home.

He'd pulled away gradually. However, Amy hadn't been able to do that. If it weren't for him, he knew that his sister would still be home under the protective eyes of their domestic staff.

"Do you ever have any regrets about the path you've taken in life?" Andrew asked. He knew he was prying, but he wanted to get to know more about Denise. She fascinated him.

With a slight shrug, she answered, "Sometimes I wish I'd stuck it out in college. At the first sign of it being distasteful, I high-tailed it out of there."

He couldn't help but laugh at the image she'd presented. "Was it the grades? Were you passing?"

"I was doing okay. My grades weren't good enough to brag about, but I could have pulled them up. I didn't know it then, but now I know I had the ability if I'd just allowed myself to mature."

"You can always go back," he said softly.

"I might do that. But now I'm pretty happy with my life just like it is. The bookstore keeps me pretty busy, and my house is just like I like it."

Andrew thought for a few minutes about what Denise had just said. She was happy with her life just like it was. Did she have room for another person? Would she be interested in striking up a relationship with him? He couldn't bring himself to come right out and ask her, so he made more small talk.

"Tell me what you like best about your house."

Grinning from ear to ear, she said, "I love the

brightness. When I wake up in the morning, I can hear the birds chirping and feel the sunlight coming through the sheer curtains I hung in my bedroom."

"You make it sound wonderful," he said wistfully.

"It is." She went on. "And the whole house is bright. I had to rip out the awful carpet and tear down the wallpaper that was too depressing to talk about. Now, everything around me is cheerful."

As is this woman, he thought. Andrew had never met a more cheerful woman in his life.

Chapter Eight

Denise was flattered that Andrew seemed so interested in everything about her. But she held herself back from expecting it to continue. Didn't most people ask a lot of questions in the beginning? Wasn't there a honeymoon phase in every relationship—even for people who were "just friends"?

Still, though, Andrew seemed different. For one thing, he was the first guy she'd met who was so attached to his little sister, although she felt like telling him to lighten up. After all, Amy was an adult—only four years younger than Denise—and she needed to learn to take care of herself, even if that meant making a few mistakes along the way.

Another thing about Andrew that was different was the fact that he didn't seem impressed by money—his or anyone else's. He took things in stride and acted like he could take it or leave it. Denise liked that. She'd learned early in life that money wasn't the most important thing in the world as long as there was enough to cover the essentials. In fact, if there was too much money in a person's bank account, too many temptations lurked.

With a sigh, Denise decided to try to relax and enjoy Andrew's attention. She'd answer his questions as they came and try not to worry. She wanted to get to know him better, but like she'd mentioned earlier in the evening, she had everything in her life just like she wanted it.

"Ready to head back?" he asked as they came to a point where they had to make a decision of which way to go.

"We probably should." Denise let out a deep sigh. She would have loved to keep walking and learning more about this man, but she didn't feel like being on the receiving end of the glances and winks she was sure would come from Bethany and Gertie.

"Amy has really taken to working at the store," Andrew said. "She told me she'd like to have her own business someday." He cleared his throat before adding, "But I'm sure she wouldn't even think of opening another bookstore in Clearview."

Denise laughed. "At the rate she's catching on, I have no doubt she'd be able to put me out of business if she did."

His face looked stricken, and Denise belted out an even heartier laugh. When he realized that she wasn't worried, he smiled back at her and reached for her hand. It felt good. Warm. Nice.

It surprised Denise that he didn't let go of her hand as they rounded the last corner and came into sight of David's and Bethany's house. She would have thought he wouldn't want Amy to get the wrong impression, but he didn't seem to care.

As they walked inside, Gertie greeted them with, "Why did you come back so early?"

Andrew shrugged. "We didn't want anyone to worry."

Denise stole a sidelong glance at him and noticed the amusement on his face. It made her heart sing. He seemed to be enjoying the family she'd adopted, and that made her happier than anything else possibly could have.

Just then, Amy came around the corner, wiping her hands on a kitchen towel. With a warm grin, looking like she'd been doing dishes all her life, she greeted her brother and Denise.

"Want some coffee?" she asked as if she was the hostess.

Andrew looked at Denise with amusement, then back at his sister. "Sure, if you're making some anyway, Amy."

Denise wondered if he was baiting his sister, but when Amy turned cheerfully back toward the kitchen, she decided everything was just fine. Andrew knew what he could and couldn't get away with saying to his sister. It was obvious that they adored each other, so if they teased, it was out of love.

They went into the living room and sat down on the sofa at Gertie's invitation. She plopped down on the chair across from them and studied them both.

Finally, when she spoke, Denise had the strange sense that Gertie was interviewing Andrew for her. She felt like she was living in a different era.

"So, how long do you think Swetson's will keep you here in town, Andrew?" Gertie asked. "I just happen to know they have offices in other parts of the country."

Andrew nodded, taking it in stride. "Yes, ma'am, they do, but I think I'll be in the Clearview office permanently. After all, this is where the entire marketing department is."

"Good, good," Gertie responded, nodding and casting a glance toward Denise. "I understand you have some personal connections with the company." Denise tensed. Why had Gertie gone there? That was way too personal.

But Andrew handled the question as a gentleman should. He nodded and openly admitted she was right. "Yes, that's how I found out about the position. But I haven't even spoken to the person who told me about it since I've been here. I suppose I should probably let him know everything is going just fine." He cleared his throat. "My immediate supervisor doesn't know anything about the stockholder, something I didn't mention in the final interview. I figured it was best if I got the job on my own merit."

Gertie nodded, "Good boy. That shows character."

He held Gertie's gaze as he said, "I don't like it when people pull strings to get jobs they're not qualified for."

Gertie grinned and winked at Denise before turning back to face Andrew. "So, Andrew, how do you like Clearview?"

"So far it seems like a nice place to live."

"Yes, it is. I've often thought it was the perfect place to raise a family. At least it was for me." Gertie kept getting closer and closer to Denise's zone of discomfort.

"I can see that," Andrew said without missing a beat. "From what I see, it's the perfect place for a lot of other things as well."

"Such as?" Gertie prompted.

"Such as starting a business," he replied.

Gertie's eyebrows shot up. "You're thinking about starting another business? Doesn't Swetson's keep you busy enough?"

He gestured toward the kitchen. "I was thinking about for my sister."

"But she works for Denise." Gertie looked appalled at such a suggestion.

Denise cleared her throat. "Most people don't want

to be a sales clerk for the rest of their lives, Gertie. I expect Amy to eventually move on."

"But not anytime soon," Andrew interjected. "I'm extremely thankful for Denise offering her that job."

Gertie grinned with satisfaction. Or was it more of a cat-that-ate-the-canary grin? Whatever it was, Denise knew that Gertie had just finished phase one of whatever it was she was doing.

"Denise is a terrific girl," Gertie said as she stood up. "She'll make someone a wonderful wife. Someone who has the sense to notice her, anyway."

Before Denise had a chance to catch her voice that had suddenly escaped, Gertie was gone. Denise gulped.

"I-I'm sorry about that," Denise told Andrew. "I didn't know how to stop her."

He took her hand in his and looked her in the eye with tenderness. "Don't worry about it. In fact, I rather enjoyed the interrogation."

"You did?" Denise's voice came out in a squeak.

Nodding, he replied, "Yes. She just told me without saying it that she loves you very much and if I want to stay on her good side, I'll treat you right. That speaks volumes for you to have someone like Gertie looking after your interest."

With a heartwarming realization of her own, Denise nodded. "It does, doesn't it?"

"And what's more," he added, "I know that if I want to keep hanging around with you, I need to keep Gertie updated on the progress of our relationship. That is, if you want to have a relationship with me."

Denise was again stunned speechless. She opened her mouth, then closed it when nothing came out. Finally, she just nodded. He laughed, with her, not at her.

When it was time to leave, Denise had the feeling she was the subject of a project among Gertie, Bethany, and David, with Gertie being the leader. And she didn't mind. She actually found it quite endearing. She knew that Gertie had played a major part in bringing Bethany and David together, and that was a match made in heaven.

Jonathan reached out for a hug as they stood at the door. He'd appeared from nowhere.

"I thought you were in bed, sport," David said to the little boy.

"I was, but I wanted to say goodbye to all our company." Jonathan rubbed his sleepy little eyes and yawned.

Denise bent over and gave him another kiss on the forehead. "As soon as we leave, you need to go right back to bed so you'll feel good tomorrow. It's Saturday, and I'd hate to see such a wonderful day go to waste with you sleeping late."

Jonathan nodded. Denise knew, based on what she'd heard from Bethany, that he never liked to sleep late on Saturdays. When he spent the night with them, he was like an alarm clock, bounding into their bedroom, bouncing on the bed, and covering them both with hugs and kisses. This is a house filled with love, Denise thought wistfully.

A Friday night in Clearview wasn't the most exciting thing in the world. But a Friday evening spent chatting with Andrew brought more excitement to Denise's life than anything she could remember, including the times she'd spent being mischievous as a teenager.

It was still early enough for Denise to read another chapter of her novel when she got home. The house was locked for the night, and the only light was in her bedroom. She changed into her gown and crawled beneath the cool sheets she'd put on her bed last night after pulling them from the dryer.

Inhaling the scent of fabric softener, Denise thought of all the things she'd done to make herself feel cozy. This sure did beat excitement any day, she thought. The only thing that would make it better was having a man to share her life with.

But that was always when her thoughts quickly turned to logic. What man would want to walk into her life and fall into place beside her, not disrupting a single thing she'd managed to build? If the relationship with Andrew developed further, would he be satisfied living in a tiny cottage, or would he expect her to live in a huge mansion where they could get lost and not see each other for days? Would he be happy having a wife who valued owning her own business and being independent? Andrew certainly didn't seem like the type to hold someone back, but Denise knew that people who grew up privileged as he did were different. They viewed life differently. Their wants became needs, and their idea of normal was way beyond what actually was normal.

With a scowl, Denise picked up her book and tried to read the words on the page. But they quickly blurred as thoughts of Andrew and his sister's mansion came to mind. She hated the darkness and dreariness of that old house.

Finally, Denise realized she couldn't concentrate on the book so she closed it and turned off the light. And after lying there with her rambling thoughts, she managed to fall asleep, a sleep that was filled with dreams.

"Did you have fun tonight, Amy?" Andrew asked his little sister. She sat in the passenger seat staring out the window, deep in thought.

She turned to him and nodded. Slowly, a smile crept across her lips. "I had the most wonderful time, Andrew. I love that family."

He sucked in a breath. He'd hoped his sister would say more about her feelings toward Denise, but she hadn't, so he'd have to ask. "Denise is almost like a part of that family, isn't she?"

Amy nodded again. "I want to be accepted like that, but it might be hard since we haven't known them very long."

"I have a feeling that doesn't matter with these people, Amy. Gertie is the most amazing woman."

"Yes, she is," Amy agreed. "She's everyone's image of the perfect grandmother."

Andrew chuckled. "Perfect isn't the word I'd use to describe Gertie, Amy, but I know what you mean. She has a certain something that draws you to her."

"Denise has that, too," Amy said as she stared at Andrew.

He felt her gaze, and when he turned his head slightly, he could see her looking at him out of the corner of his eye. How should he respond? he wondered.

"Denise seems like a nice person," he offered as casually as he could manage.

Amy let her head fall back, and she laughed heartily. "Nice is an understatement, Andrew. I think you know it." He noticed when he came to a stop sign that she was grinning from ear to ear. "You like her, don't you?"

"Yes," he replied, knowing it was pointless to deny his feelings. "Very much. At least what I know of her, I like."

"Well, then, I hope the two of you get plenty of opportunities to get to know each other."

"You know her pretty well, after spending so much time in the store with her, don't you?" he asked, hoping he didn't sound too anxious.

"Sort of," Amy replied. "She's pretty much all business while we're in there. Friendly, though. All her customers seem to like working with her. I hope they start asking for me soon."

"I'm sure they will, Amy."

Andrew was proud of his sister for having gotten this job, and he saw that being a responsible woman agreed with her. He hadn't been sure how she'd deal with the changes, but what he saw in her was remarkable. She'd transformed from being mousy and quiet to stepping up and speaking for herself. That might not be much for most people, he thought, but for Amy it was a lot.

"If and when I decide to go into business for myself, I want to be as happy as Denise."

Andrew reached out and patted his sister on the shoulder. "I'm sure you will be, Amy. Just make sure it's something you enjoy."

She let out a big sigh. "The only problem is, I can't see myself owning any business besides a bookstore, and the last thing this town needs is another bookstore. As it is, I think Denise barely earns a living with Carson's. It's always crowded, but I wouldn't want to do anything to jeopardize the way she earns a living."

"We'll have to think of something else, then," Andrew said. He figured that since Amy had just started testing her wings, they had plenty of time to decide what kind of business she wanted.

* * *

Denise was already inside the store when Amy arrived the next morning. "Want me to set up for the story hour?" Amy asked.

"Sure, Amy," Denise replied. "That would be great. I've got to count the deposit again. I was in such a hurry to get out of here last night, the cash register didn't balance with the deposit."

Amy moved around, getting the books ready and arranging the props they used for the story hour. Denise had started using puppets to help tell the stories, and it had delighted the children, so they continued.

It took almost half an hour for Denise to find the error, but when she did, she let out a sigh of relief. It had been hers, and it was minor, but she hated being off by even a few dollars.

"Find it?" Amy asked as Denise joined her.

Denise nodded. "That's the only part about the business I don't like."

"I thought Bethany kept the books for you."

"She does, but I do the deposits every night. She enters everything on the ledger once a week."

"We had a good time last night," Amy said. "I love the way David and Bethany made me feel like part of the family."

With a chuckle, Denise nodded. "They have a way of doing that. Bethany and I go way back. She didn't exactly have it easy growing up."

"She didn't?" Amy asked innocently. "That's hard to imagine with a grandmother like Gertie."

"Gertie was always wonderful, but Bethany's parents divorced when she was a little girl. She never saw her father again, but she heard stories that upset her. Her mother was always so sad, and then after Bethany got settled in her job in Atlanta, her mother died. It was a rough blow when Gertie had her stroke."

"Is that why Gertie moved into that tiny apartment?"

"No, she was already there when she had her stroke. It's a good thing she didn't have that big house to take care of when it happened."

Amy nodded. "It's a warm house, but I can imagine how difficult it would be for one elderly woman to have to maintain."

Denise nodded. "David had quite a few repairs to make after he bought it. I'm just glad he's the one Bethany met and fell in love with. They're so perfect for each other, and she gets to live in the house she's always loved."

Amy cast a glance toward Denise, then quickly looked away. "You said you grew up in Allendale. Was it always like it is now?"

Without her having to say it, Denise knew what Amy was talking about. Allendale was not only the ritziest neighborhood in town, it was stuffy and stodgy.

"It's always been the most exclusive neighborhood," Denise replied, trying hard to keep her voice from betraying her disdain for her old stomping grounds, "but I'd prefer something a little less . . . a little less . . ." Her voice trailed off as she tried to think of some way to describe Allendale without criticizing where her employee lived.

Amy nodded. "I think I know what you mean. You like the warmth of David's and Bethany's house, and you like the brightness of your place. Allendale is nothing like either of them."

Grinning to be let off the hook so easily, Denise nodded. "Exactly."

Amy continued to look at Denise with curiosity. "I'm still hoping you'll help me brighten my house up a bit. I know it'll never be perfect, but at least I might be able to do a few things to make it nicer."

Nicer? Denise thought about that word. To her, nicer meant something completely different from what she imagined Amy was used to. But she couldn't turn Amy down.

"I'll be glad to do whatever I can," she said.

"Can we get started soon?" Amy asked. "I don't want to keep going into that dark kitchen. It depresses me."

Kitchens were Denise's favorite places. Brightening up Amy's kitchen would be a pleasure.

"Just let me know when you want to get started, and I'll be glad to help."

"How about next week?" Amy asked.

"Sounds good."

The children had started filing in. Since this story

hour had become a regular event at Carson's Bookstore, they all knew what to do. Denise went to the back room and got a box of graham crackers and a tray of apple juice with half-filled paper cups. She'd had a few accidents with the children spilling their juice, but she considered that just normal wear and tear on the carpet. It wasn't anything to worry about. The first time that had happened, though, she'd noticed how Amy acted like it was the end of the world. Her household staff must have been extremely repressive, Denise thought as she blotted the spill with a towel.

It hadn't taken long for Amy to learn to relax about insignificant things like apple juice messes and graham cracker crumbs. She'd learned to ignore little jabs and squirms from the kids, and she'd become a marvelous storyteller. Denise was thrilled about that because it freed her up to do other things in the store.

The children sat and listened to Amy for the next hour. Denise helped their parents with book selections. She was engrossed in explaining the layout of the store to a new parent when she felt the gaze of someone from the front door.

Denise quickly glanced up and spotted Andrew standing there looking back and forth from his sister, who was surrounded by children at her feet, to Denise, who was still talking to a parent. She smiled, then turned her attention back to the woman.

As soon as Denise was free, Andrew quickly made

his way over to her. “Quite an operation you’ve got going here. I can see why you’re a success.”

“I care about my customers,” Denise said as she tried to hide her excitement at seeing him. She hadn’t expected Andrew to come this morning because Amy was scheduled to work until mid-afternoon.

“Well, I can see that you’re busy. I just happened to be in the neighborhood, so I thought I’d stop by and see if you’d like to go out with me after you close.” Andrew had asked her out so casually, it almost didn’t register with her.

When she realized he was waiting for an answer, she gulped and said, “I’d love to.”

“And how about church in the morning?” he asked. “Is that too much too soon?”

Chapter Nine

"Church?" Denise asked, not believing what was happening.

"Yes, church," Andrew replied. "You *do* go to New Hope, don't you?"

"Well, yes, but I didn't know you were going there." Denise glanced over at Amy, who was taking it all in with a grin from her side of the room. Denise wondered if Amy could hear what they were talking about.

"Amy and I are going to start tomorrow, and I was wondering if I could pick you up to go with us."

Denise took a step back and looked down at the counter. She wasn't sure if he wanted her to go as his date or if he just wanted her there for moral support for Amy, who'd admitted she hadn't been to church in years.

What did it matter, though? Either way, it should be a pleasant experience.

She looked back up at Andrew and forced a smile. "Sure, I'd love to go with you."

"Now that that's settled, how about tonight? Maybe we can take in a movie, then grab a bite to eat. I know this town closes early, so it won't be a late night."

Denise chuckled. "You got that right." She only had to think for a couple seconds before she nodded. "I'd love to go out with you tonight, Andrew."

They made plans for him to meet her at her house half an hour after she closed the store. That way she'd have a chance to change clothes and freshen up a bit.

"But what about Amy?" Denise asked. "I thought you didn't like leaving her alone in the house."

"Bethany told me I could bring Amy over there to help her bake and watch Jonathan. Apparently it's pretty hard to do both."

Denise nodded. "I can only imagine." And she could only imagine how eager Bethany was to do whatever it took to get her and Andrew together. It seemed that all Bethany could talk about was how wonderful it was to be married.

After Andrew left, Amy ambled over to Denise and stared at her with wide eyes. "Did my brother ask you out?"

"Yes, he did. Why didn't you tell me he was going to come in here and do this?" Denise asked.

Amy shrugged. "It wasn't my place to do that. Besides, we were busy from the moment I got here."

That was true, Denise thought. There were very few slow times in the store on Saturday.

"Well, what did you tell him?" Amy continued to watch Denise with those wide eyes.

"I said I'd go."

Amy clasped her hands together and started jumping around like an eager child. "This is so much fun!" Then, she calmed down and shifted her feet uncomfortably. "Denise?" she asked with a little hesitation.

"What, Amy?" For some reason, Denise had the feeling she was about to be asked something important.

"Is it possible . . ." Her voice trailed off as she looked away for a few seconds.

"Is it possible, what?" Denise asked.

Amy turned and looked Denise squarely in the eye. "Is it possible for you to take me to get my driver's permit next week?"

Denise frowned for a moment. "I don't mind. But why doesn't Andrew do it?"

"Well," Amy began as she moved her hands along the edge of the counter, "he's not all that excited about me doing this. But I really want to drive. My daddy even offered to get me a car if I got my license."

"He did?" Denise was surprised. She'd thought that

Andrew's overprotectiveness of Amy was an extension of their parents' desires.

"Yes," Amy squealed with excitement. "And I've already got it picked out. It's a little red one over at the dealership on the other side of town. It's so pretty!"

Denise remembered her first car and how she felt about it. There was never anything that compared to it since. "I suppose I can take you. Do you have the rulebook so you can study?"

Amy shrugged. "I used to have my permit, but I let it expire. I figured I could remember all the things from that test."

After she let out a long breath, Denise looked directly at Amy and said, "I'll take you under one condition, Amy."

"Sure," Amy said suspiciously. "What's that?"

"You have to get the book and study. No, I tell you what. I'll get the book for you. I can stop by the Department of Motor Vehicles Monday morning on my way over here if you can open the store for me."

"You'd do that for me?" Amy asked.

"Of course. But you have to study every page of that book. It's not the same as it was a few years ago."

"I'll do whatever it takes," Amy agreed. "But please don't tell my brother. I want to surprise him."

"Did Coach Simmons ever get ahold of you?" Denise asked, now remembering that she'd called him and told him he had a potential student for after-school instruction.

Amy nodded. “He told me we can practice driving as soon as I get my permit.”

They spent the rest of the day waiting on customers and straightening the store. It was an average Saturday, so they didn’t have too much to do, other than the routine.

When Andrew came to Denise’s house after work, she watched through the window as he walked up the sidewalk. He was carrying a bouquet of fresh-cut flowers, which touched her heart. Andrew was a really nice man, and she hated having to keep Amy’s secret from him. But this matter of Amy’s license didn’t concern her, so she had no business telling him anything about it. Amy was an adult, and she was Denise’s friend. She knew she’d have to keep the subject off his sister, so she’d planned a few conversation starters and diversions.

They had a wonderful time at the movie. It was something she’d been meaning to see, but hadn’t gotten around to it.

“Ready for a little drive out of town?” Andrew asked.

Denise crinkled her forehead. “Where?”

He shrugged. “I thought it would be a nice change of pace to go to Plattsville for a steak.”

“The Pine Room?” Denise asked, her eyebrows raised.

Andrew nodded. "I heard they have the best steaks in the county."

"They definitely do," Denise agreed. "That's where my parents used to take me to celebrate important things."

He squeezed her hand. "Then let's consider this a celebration of the first date of what I hope will be many."

The way he looked at her melted her to her toes. Andrew was very charming, and she didn't know anyone else quite like him. He didn't seem to mind expressing his feelings toward her, but she was still unsure of where this whole thing between them was going. They were very alike in some ways but worlds apart in others. For one thing, what would he say once he found out she was taking Amy for her permit? That might be the last time he ever spoke to her. Denise wasn't the type to let that stand in her way of doing what she thought was right, though, so turning Amy down wasn't an option.

All the way to Plattsville, Denise did her best to keep the conversation light and away from Amy. But she could only do that for so long.

"Jonathan is a very rambunctious little boy, isn't he?" Andrew asked.

Denise nodded. "He's a little more active than most, but he's basically a good kid."

"Bethany said that when she tries to bake, he likes to get into the sugar and flour. Sometimes she has to abandon what she's doing to give him the attention he needs," Andrew continued.

"Yes, that's true."

"That's why she was thrilled to have Amy come over to keep him busy," Andrew continued. "Amy's almost like a child herself."

Denise had to bite her tongue to keep from telling Andrew that his sister was a grown woman who needed to be treated like one. It was hard, though. He didn't see her that way at all, and Denise feared that he never would, in spite of some of the comments he'd made to the contrary.

"She's good with kids," Denise said.

Nodding, Andrew replied. "That she is. I worry about her all the time."

"Why do you worry so much?"

With a shrug, Andrew said, "Ever since she was a baby, she's been pampered. My parents gave her everything she wanted, and the servants waited on her hand and foot to please my mom and dad."

"Did they do that for you, too?" Denise asked.

"No, I was different. I was the type to try everything on my own, shoving everyone out of my way in the process. I think my dad gave up on me a long time ago." Andrew chuckled. "But he was proud of me for finishing college and getting my first job on my own."

"Don't most people do that?" Denise had turned and was studying his profile as he drove.

He shook his head. "Not in the social circle my

parents are in. Most of their friends' kids have had their hands out, taking everything their daddies have to give. But I want more in life than that."

"More? Like more things than your dad offers?"

"No, not really. What I mean is that I want to make it on my own, regardless of who my parents are. They have a hard time understanding that sometimes, but I think my father's proud. My mother keeps begging me to take a job in Nashville, but my dad tells her I need to do this. My first job wasn't so difficult for them to accept once they got used to the idea."

"Was that the job you had before this one?"

He nodded. "It was a pretty good situation, too. I'd been promoted several times, and the company was in a growth mode. But I felt like I needed to get away, so when my dad's friend called and told me about Swetson's I considered this the opportunity I needed to make my own way in a place where no one knew who I was."

"What did your parents say?"

He chuckled. "My mom cried, and my dad questioned the sanity of it."

Denise agreed. "I'm surprised your parents let Amy come with you to Clearview."

"To be honest with you, so am I," he stated flatly. "But she didn't get to come unless we agreed to certain conditions."

"The house," Denise said.

He nodded. "That and a few other things." Letting

out a long-suffering sigh, he said, "I have to look after her and make sure she stays out of harm's way."

"That shouldn't be too hard in Clearview. There's not a whole lot she can get into."

With a cute but wicked grin, he cast a quick glance Denise's way. "But that didn't stop you and Bethany when you were kids, did it?"

Denise blushed. "Well, no, but we were teenagers. That's quite different from a twenty-three-year-old woman who's responsible." She pulled her lips between her teeth before adding, "And Amy is a very responsible woman, Andrew, in spite of what you might think."

"Maybe so," he said pensively.

Now was the time for them to change the subject, Denise thought. The conversation seemed to be edging dangerously close to the very thing she didn't want to discuss—Amy's freedom and independence.

"So, how do you like Clearview so far?" Denise asked, hoping he'd take the bait.

He thought for a moment before he replied, "I'm pleasantly surprised at how much I really do like it. It's a peaceful town with very pleasant people."

"And a few eccentric ones, too," Denise added.

"I wasn't going to mention Gertie Chalmers, but yes, a few eccentric ones, too."

"Gertie just happens to be the nicest, warmest, funniest person I've ever known in my life," Denise said in defense of her best friend's grandmother.

"Oh, don't get me wrong," he said, his face registering dismay at how she'd misinterpreted what he'd said. "Gertie is adorable, and my sister loves her. It's just that you never know what she's going to come up with next."

Denise tossed her hair over her shoulder as she belted out a laugh. "That's probably what I like most about her. She's unpredictable."

"Yes, she's unpredictable, all right." Andrew thought for a moment. "But then again, so are you."

Chapter Ten

Denise had to do a double-take to make sure she heard him right. He had a smirk on his face that let her know she had. “What was that supposed to mean?”

Andrew reached out, taking her hand in his for a moment. He squeezed it, then let go. “Nothing bad, I assure you. It’s just that you have a mind of your own, and you say some things that throw me for a loop.”

She let out a sigh of resignation. “I have been compared to Gertie in the past. People tell me we’re like two peas in a pod and that I’m more like her than Bethany is.”

“Maybe that’s why Bethany likes you so much.”

“Probably,” Denise agreed. “And I like Bethany because she has the ability to keep me grounded. We got into all sorts of things back in high school, but if it weren't for her, I would have taken it a step further and probably wound up in a whole lot more trouble."

"I'm glad the two of you were good for each other," Andrew said. "And now that you've experienced all those things, I think you'll be good for my sister."

There he was, bringing the subject around to Amy again, Denise thought. She couldn't seem to do anything to stop him. And his last comment made her very nervous. Would he still think she was good for Amy once he found out she was helping with the driver's license?

"I hope you like the Pine Room," Denise said as they arrived in Plattsville.

"I'm sure I will, based on what I've heard," he said as he drove down the only street in town. "I'm just surprised at how small this town is."

"There are a lot of small towns around here," Denise said. "Why are you surprised?"

He shrugged. "The Pine Room is pretty well known. I imagined it being in a little larger city than this."

Denise bit back the sarcastic comment she was tempted to make. This was one time she needed to hold back, although she didn't have much experience doing that. Most of the time she said what was on her mind. Her parents used to lecture her about her mouth and how she'd get herself into all sorts of hot water if she didn't learn to refrain. They were right, especially now.

The dinner experience couldn't have been better.

Andrew stopped discussing his sister, and he concentrated on her and how she'd come to be the owner of a bookstore.

"I admire you for doing what you did," he said. "It couldn't have been easy."

She shrugged as she put her napkin on the table beside her plate. "I never really thought about how difficult it was. I just went after what I wanted like I always do—full steam ahead."

"Another thing I admire about you," he said.

"How was your steak?" Denise asked, trying to change the subject, now that he'd fallen into the trap of issuing one compliment after another. It made her uncomfortable when people did that.

"I have to admit," he said in amazement, "it's one of the best meals I've ever had."

Denise felt smug about that admission. He'd appeared a little reluctant to follow through with their plans when he'd seen the exterior of the building. It was painted a drab beige, and the only sign was above the door. But the interior was filled with the finest furnishings, white tablecloths, and exquisite chandeliers. The difference was like night and day.

As they were leaving the restaurant, Andrew cast a glance behind them. "I wonder why they don't do something to spruce up the outside of this place."

"Maybe because they don't have to. People accept it as it is."

Andrew sighed and looked at her out of the corner

of his eye. "Why do I feel like you're trying to tell me something?"

She shrugged. "Maybe because you feel like I *should* be telling you something."

"Touché," he said with a grin.

Conversation all the way back to Clearview was light and fun. She couldn't remember laughing so much on a date. Andrew had a wonderful sense of humor about everything but his sister, and that was probably because he felt more like her father than her brother.

He pulled up in her driveway and stopped the car. When he turned to face her, Denise knew she was about to be kissed. Her stomach did that old flip-flop thing it used to do back when she was a teenager.

As their lips touched, Denise could tell he was holding his breath. The kiss was brief, but it felt right. This was the first time in her life Denise could remember feeling like she could be with a man indefinitely.

Andrew walked Denise to her door and brushed his lips across her forehead. "I want to see you again," he said in a husky voice.

"Of course, you'll see me again," she said with a nervous giggle. "Your sister works for me, and whenever you need to buy a book, you have to come to Carson's. I'm the only game in town as far as reading material goes."

He chuckled as he pulled away. "That's right. You have a monopoly on the written word. But that's not what I'm talking about. I want to be with you, take you out to movies, go for long walks with you . . ."

Denise's heart pounded nearly out of control. She opened her mouth, but words wouldn't come out. All she could do was nod.

"See you tomorrow morning?" he said as he tilted his head forward toward hers.

Again, she nodded.

After she unlocked her front door, Andrew gave her hand a squeeze and left. She watched him leave from her living room window. It felt so right to be with him, and now she had some memories to keep her company as she lay in bed, unable to sleep.

It took her half the night to fall into a dream-filled sleep. But when her alarm clock went off to announce that it was time to get up, Denise felt amazingly rested. She showered, dressed, and was ready long before Andrew and Amy were due to arrive. That was unlike Denise, who generally kept people waiting while she dawdled in her room, deciding on what jewelry or shoes to wear.

When they picked her up for church, Amy was waiting in the back seat of Andrew's car. Denise felt strange getting in the front, knowing that Amy was by herself in the back. But Amy didn't seem to mind.

Church was fun, especially since Denise got to introduce the new people in town to some of her old friends. Gertie was in rare form after the services, too, and she had Denise, Andrew, and Amy in stitches.

They were standing outside by one of the concrete picnic tables when Bethany came up from behind and grabbed Denise's arm. Denise jumped. When she realized who it was, she smiled.

"I kept trying to get your attention, Denise, but you were preoccupied," Bethany said, nodding toward Andrew who was standing about ten feet away, talking to one of the other church members.

"Yeah, I guess you could say that," Denise said. "Did you want something?"

Bethany let out a breath and nodded. With a slight hesitation, she said, "We've got Jonathan this weekend, but David and I have to be somewhere this afternoon. Would you mind taking him home with you?"

"Of course I don't mind," Denise said. "What are friends for?"

Bethany hugged her. "I really appreciate this, you know. He seems to always want to be with us, but sometimes it gets difficult when we need to do something."

"I can imagine," Denise said. "Being in the ministry has more than enough demands."

"You can say that again," Bethany said good-naturedly.

Jonathan sat in the back seat with Amy and chattered non-stop all the way to Denise's house. When they arrived, Denise invited them all in. "I can make sandwiches, and we can have a picnic in the backyard."

"Picnic?" Jonathan squealed. "I love picnics! Do those frogs still live in that pond in your yard?"

"That ditch?" Denise said with a chuckle. "I think so." Then, she turned to Andrew and explained. "Jonathan loves frogs."

Amy made a face and said, "Eewww."

"Frogs are cool," Jonathan said in defense of his favorite creatures. "One day they're tadpoles, and the next they're frogs. And they like to eat bugs."

Denise chuckled at the reasons Jonathan gave for thinking frogs were cool. Amy's reaction was priceless, too. Apparently, she'd never collected outdoor creatures and kept them in mayonnaise jars under her bed like she and Bethany had. But then again, Amy probably never went outside unless she had a nanny with her, and only then in a starched dress.

"I'll show you my favorite frog if he's still there. His name is Freddie," Jonathan said to Amy, his expression sincere and serious. "He's a granddaddy."

"Freddie?" Amy shuddered. "You name the frogs?"

"Of course," Jonathan said. "Everyone should have a name."

"Of course," Amy replied.

Andrew watched the road as he drove, but Denise could see that he was amused. "Did you ever collect frogs?" she asked him.

"I did once, but my mother made one of the servants get rid of them."

"Too bad," Denise said. "There's nothing better for a kid than to appreciate nature."

"It's not too late to learn, though, is it?" he asked.

Denise felt a tug at her heart once again. "No, it's never too late to learn." She suspected there was more than one meaning behind his question.

When they arrived at Denise's house, she gave Jonathan strict instructions to stay in the yard. He was too excited about the picnic to behave in the house.

Amy smiled. "I'll stay with him," she offered. "That is, if you don't need my help."

Denise nodded. "Trust me, you'll be helping me if you're with Jonathan. I won't have to worry about him."

The smile on Amy's face showed her gratitude, but Denise was confused. Why was Amy so pleased?

"You just gave my sister the best compliment anyone ever has," Andrew explained when they got to the kitchen.

"I did?"

"Yes. I think you're the first person who has ever given her this much responsibility."

"She's a smart woman. She can handle a lot more responsibility than this. Plus, she's good with kids."

Andrew sighed. "I can see that. I never realized it before, though, and it takes me by surprise."

"Why?"

He shrugged. "I don't know. I guess because I never

thought of her as being an adult. I always saw her as a child."

"You're gonna have to stop doing that, you know," Denise said before she had a chance to think first.

Andrew visibly stiffened. "Yes, I'm sure."

Suddenly, the conversation between them became stilted. Denise knew why, too. She'd insulted Andrew and stepped over the line with him, butting into his relationship between him and his sister. But he needed to back off so Amy could grow. He didn't seem to want to do that.

Denise tried to tell herself that his sudden aloofness didn't bother her, but it did. He remained in the kitchen, but his mind was obviously somewhere else. When she finished piling the lettuce and tomatoes on the sandwiches, she topped them off with another slice of bread, and arranged them on a platter that she handed to Andrew.

"Why don't you take these outside? I'll bring a pitcher of lemonade."

He did as he was told. Denise watched as he carried the platter to the wooden picnic table David had made for her as a housewarming gift. Jonathan ran over to the table, then stood there with his nose wrinkled.

Denise quickly gathered paper cups and the pitcher of lemonade that she'd made the day before and carried it outside. "Aren't you hungry, Jonathan?" she asked.

With his nose still wrinkled, he shook his head. "I don't like lettuce and tomatoes."

"Oh, I forgot," Denise said. She went back inside and grabbed the garbage can and held it out for him. "Just take what you don't like off the sandwich and eat the rest."

Andrew glared at her. "Lettuce and tomatoes are good for him. He should eat it. He needs his vegetables."

Denise had to make a decision right then and there, knowing that no matter what she did, someone wouldn't agree. With a slight hesitation, she held out the garbage can and looked at Andrew. "One meal without vegetables won't hurt him."

Amy quickly glanced over at her brother with a stunned expression on her face. She'd probably never dared do anything he didn't approve of. But Denise could do whatever she pleased, she told herself. This was her house, and Jonathan was in her care. She'd made her decision.

But Jonathan had picked up on the tension, and he pulled his sandwich back. "I'll eat it," he said quietly.

Denise felt her body become tense. Jonathan seemed to be worried about causing friction, probably because of the relationship between his parents being so shaky. He didn't want to cause the same thing between Andrew and Denise.

At first, she wasn't sure what to do, but she decided

to let the subject drop. It wasn't worth the worry of standing her ground just to prove a point.

Amy also sensed the tension, and she kept casting angry glances at Andrew. Denise didn't like the blanket of dissension that had fallen over the group. But no matter how hard she tried to lighten things up, the air remained heavy with hard feelings.

Jonathan picked up on it, too. He showed Amy where the frogs were, but he kept glancing over his shoulder at Denise and Andrew, who were picking up the remnants of the picnic to carry them back to the kitchen.

After Amy and Andrew left, Jonathan turned to Denise with tears in his eyes and said, "I didn't mean to make you mad, Denise. I won't ever do that again."

"Oh, honey," Denise said as she hugged the little boy, "don't worry about anything. You didn't do anything wrong. We're just tired and grouchy."

"But I made Andrew mad at you."

"No, you didn't do that. He's just not used to being around little boys, that's all."

Jonathan sniffled. "But he was a little boy once."

"I'm not so sure about that," Denise said, the realization hitting her like a ton of bricks.

That was the problem with Andrew. He'd never been allowed to just be a kid. From when he was very young, Andrew had been expected to do certain things, to perform a certain way, to act like a little man, just to please his demanding parents. Denise didn't think that made them bad parents, just misguided.

Fortunately for her, both of her parents grew up in middle-class homes, where their lives had been pretty normal. When she came into the world, she didn't have a set of rigid rules to live by.

The Carson family had employed a maid and extra help when they entertained, but that was only after Denise's father had made his money in banking. He'd started out at the very bottom of his career ladder, and through his good business sense and being in the right place at the right time, he'd managed to work his way to the top. And he never let her forget her roots, something Denise was extremely grateful for, especially now that she'd seen how things could have been. Amy's biggest problem was that she'd never been allowed to be in touch with the real world.

Bethany picked up Jonathan a couple hours later. "I can't thank you enough," Bethany told Denise. "As it was, Emily was fussy, and we had to leave early."

"Jonathan's a good boy," Denise said, making sure he heard her. "He was no trouble at all."

After they left, Denise flopped onto the sofa and drew in a deep breath. She needed a little time alone to think things over. Her feelings were coming in too fast, and she knew she had to take a time-out, or she'd explode with anxiety, something she'd never suffered from before.

The next day, Amy came rushing into the store with

her driver's manual in her hands. "I want you to quiz me on the first part, Denise," she said. "Mondays are always slow, so I didn't think you'd mind."

Denise was amazed at how much Amy had learned already. "Does Andrew know about this?"

"No, not yet," Amy admitted.

"How did you study without him seeing you?"

Amy shrugged. "I told him I was tired, and I went to my room early. I've only read over it a couple times."

"This information is full of numbers and statistics. You learned all of it by just reading over it a couple times last night?" Denise asked in amazement.

Amy nodded with a grin on her face. "I never really had much trouble in school. Studying and learning came easy to me. It was the social part I had trouble with."

Denise marveled at how smart Amy was. And it troubled her that she had so much untapped potential. She now realized that it was up to her as Amy's employer to give the young woman the gentle nudge she needed to get where she wanted to go.

For the remainder of the day, whenever they reached a slow time, Denise drilled Amy on the part she'd studied. That night, Denise instructed her to learn the information in the rest of the book. "You already know the first part, practically by heart. It won't take long before you have this whole thing down pat."

She was right. By the next day, Amy had the entire book memorized.

"You're very smart, Amy," Denise said.

Amy beamed with pride at that compliment. "My teachers have always told me that, but it means so much more coming from you."

"There are so many things we can learn from places we least expect it."

Nodding, Amy said, "I know that now." She reached up and patted her hair, recapturing a strand with one of the pins that had slipped.

Denise took a long, hard look at Amy and found herself wondering something else. "Have you thought about the new hairstyle we were talking about?"

Amy adamantly shook her head. "I've thought about it, but I'd never get away with it."

"And why not?" Denise asked. "Bethany and I used to experiment with different hair styles when we had sleepovers. I thought all girls did that."

"I've never been to a sleepover," Amy admitted.

Chapter Eleven

"You've never been to a sleepover?" Denise asked in disbelief. "I thought that was part of growing up. All kids go to sleepovers."

"My parents didn't want me to go. They told me that bad things happen at sleepovers."

"Bad things? Like what?" Denise asked. She was shocked that anyone would tell a child something like that.

Amy shrugged. "They never said."

"And you took their word for it?" Man, Denise knew she'd never take her own parents' word for anything if it didn't make sense to her. But then her parents had always encouraged her to think for herself, something she remembered Amy's parents didn't do.

"I didn't have a choice," Amy said solemnly. "But

now I'm curious. What actually happens at sleep-overs?"

Denise suddenly got a wild idea. She'd have a sleepover. But who would she invite? Definitely Amy and Bethany, but she wanted to have more people than that. This was one of those things that the saying "the more the merrier" was made for.

There was Connie at the Cut 'n Curl. She was quite a bit younger than Denise, so they'd never socialized much. But so was Amy. As she thought about it, the names of several women came to mind. She'd have to do it in a couple weeks, though, because she had offered to help out with Jonathan again next weekend.

Amy was thrilled at the very idea of a sleepover. "Just think, I'll finally get to see what it is I've been missing all my life." Suddenly, a dark cloud seemed to settle over her. She looked crestfallen.

"What's wrong?" Denise asked.

"What if Andrew doesn't let me go?"

Denise felt like she might explode. "Not let you go? He can't tell you what to do, Amy. You're a grown woman."

Amy's chest rose and fell as she took a couple deep breaths. Slowly, a smile crept across her face, and she nodded. "Yes, I am, and no one can tell me what to do."

"That's the spirit." Denise patted Amy on the shoulder with pride. "As long as it doesn't involve him, you're in charge of what happens to yourself."

People started coming into the store, and they got busy helping customers and ringing up sales. At the end of the day, Amy turned to Denise and announced, "I'm going to be ready to take my written driver's test by the end of the week, but I don't know how I'll get to the Department of Motor Vehicles. Andrew still doesn't know about it."

"You're not going to tell him?" Denise asked.

"I was thinking I'd surprise him after I got it."

Nodding, Denise agreed. "Yes, that's a good idea." There was nothing Andrew could do about it then. "Maybe I can take you some morning before we open."

Amy's eyes lit up again. "Would you? Are you sure you don't mind?"

"Of course I don't mind."

The look of gratitude on Amy's face was almost more than Denise could bear. She knew Andrew would be furious with her for what he'd consider interference from someone who didn't have an interest in his sister. But she did care about Amy. Denise knew that Amy was not only very smart, she was beautiful, too. And she had such a cute personality that was itching to come out. All Denise was trying to do was help her realize her full potential.

Memories from high school flashed through Denise's mind. She'd seen the same thing in Bethany, even when they were children, and she'd encouraged Bethany to let her feelings out. It was hard, and it took time, but eventually Bethany became more outspoken and assertive, something that bugged Gertie out of her skull. Denise had to laugh at some of the reactions from Bethany's grandmother. The only thing that had calmed Gertie down was when Mr. Chalmers, Bethany's grandfather, had reminded her that she was the exact same way when she was a teenager.

Still, though, Gertie had warned Denise that she was watching her like a hawk. It had taken becoming an adult before Denise earned Gertie's respect. Now, they were very good friends, something Denise thought would never happen.

After she and Amy closed the store, Denise went home and started placing calls to old friends for the sleepover. All the women had been caught by surprise on this one, but no one turned her down.

"That's a great idea, Denise," Connie said. "Only you would think of something like that."

"Bring your combs and scissors, too, because I have a feeling we'll be doing a makeover," Denise advised.

"Ooh, fun! I love makeovers. I hope you asked Phyllis to come, too. She's the best aesthetician we have at the shop, and she works wonders with makeup."

"Good idea," Denise said. "I'll call her next."

After they hung up, Denise called and invited Phyllis, who squealed with delight. "I can't wait to get my hands on her. She's got that peaches and cream complexion that's so much fun to work with."

Denise saved Bethany for last, since she wanted to talk to her for a while. "You're what?"

"I'm having a sleepover," Denise repeated.

"That's what I thought you said. Are you out of your mind? What will a bunch of women do at a sleep-over?"

Denise chuckled. "One thing I know we won't be doing is rolling people's yards."

Bethany giggled. "I should hope not. Can you imagine what people would say if we got caught?"

"Hmm," Denise said. "Maybe we should. It would be a kick to watch the sheriff arrest the preacher's wife."

"Don't get any funny ideas, Denise," Bethany warned good-naturedly. "But I have to admit, it does sound like fun. Want me to bring some board games?"

"You can if you want, but I have a feeling this will be more of a gab-fest than anything else. I wanted to do something to make Amy feel more a part of Clear-view."

Bethany groaned. "I knew you were up to something, Denise. What else do you have in mind?"

"Me?" Denise asked, her voice an octave higher than usual. "You think I have an ulterior motive?"

"I *know* you have an ulterior motive. We've been friends for a long time. Remember?"

"Yeah, that's true. I guess I'd better 'fess up. I've invited Connie and Phyllis to help Amy realize her full potential." Denise inspected the back of her hand while she waited for the reprimand from her best friend.

Instead she got the total opposite reaction. "I think that's a great idea. David and I have been hoping Amy would pull out of her shell."

"Really?" Denise said. "Then you'll be glad to know she's going for her driver's permit this week."

"Be careful, Denise," Bethany warned. "Andrew likes you, but he doesn't want other people pushing Amy too hard."

"I'm not pushing her," Denise said in defense. "I'm just giving her a gentle nudge."

Bethany chuckled. "Yeah, like you did me."

"That was different."

"Just don't nudge her over the cliff, Denise. Andrew will never forgive you."

Denise sniffed. "I have no idea what you're talking about. Amy's not going to do anything she doesn't already want to."

After an audible sigh, Bethany replied, "I'm sure you're right. But don't expect Andrew to see it that way."

"I've already thought of that," Denise said. "And I'm willing to take the chance."

After they got off the phone, Denise made herself a sandwich and a bowl of canned soup. She was both mentally and physically exhausted, but she needed to go for a brisk walk before changing into her nightclothes. Otherwise, the stress and excitement might wear her down.

There was nothing Denise enjoyed more than walking through the residential streets of Clearview in the early evening, during the dinner hour, when she could smell the aroma of food cooking and hear the sounds of children playing outside while they waited. It was a special time that reminded her of her own youth.

Denise considered herself fortunate for having had the best of both worlds—the nice things money could buy and the earthiness of a mother who kept her from having her head in a cloud. Although her family had more than enough material possessions, her parents had instilled in her the value of knowing where it came from and not thinking she deserved special privileges just because of it. Her father spent plenty of time with her, making her feel like a special member of the family, but he warned her that others were special, too.

When she'd become a teenager, Denise had developed a wild streak that had her parents worried, and rightfully so. She'd done a few things that earned her the reputation of being a spoiled rich girl with too much time on her hands.

Her father had caught wind of some of her escapades, and he'd spent hours lecturing her. But she was rebellious and kept on doing whatever she wanted and feeling guilty later. That didn't stop her from doing it again, though. One thing she was grateful for was the fact that her parents never gave up on her. Too bad they were gone now and couldn't see how successful she was in business. They'd be proud.

Denise wasn't proud of her past, but there was nothing she could do about it now. It was history. And she'd learned a lot of things about herself. She also knew that when she had kids, she'd have some personal experience to pull from when warning about all the things they shouldn't do because she'd done them all. Well, not all, but most of them. She'd never stolen anything or physically hurt anyone. In fact, the worst things had been more destructive to herself than anyone else, like staying out past curfew and driving around town with the radio turned full blast. To some adults, including her parents and Gertie, that was bad enough.

After she got back from her walk, Denise took a quick shower and crawled into bed with a book. Life was good, and it was about to get even better.

Amy came into the store the next morning, her eyes wide with excitement. "I'm ready for my test," she announced. "Can we go tomorrow?"

"Sure," Denise said. "But you're not scheduled to work today."

"I know. I have a little shopping to do in town, so I wanted to stop by and see you first."

That was sweet, Denise thought. She knew that Amy looked up to her and enjoyed being in the store. "Want some tea?"

"Not today. There's a sale at the boutique, and I want to be the first one in line."

Denise chuckled. Amy had so much money in her bank account, she didn't have to wait for sales. But she enjoyed the thrill of the victory when she beat someone else to the twenty-five percent off on a pretty outfit.

"Sounds like fun," Denise said. "Let me know if there's anything good."

"I will," Amy called over her shoulder as she left the store.

Andrew came in a little later. "Wanna go to lunch?"

Denise shook her head. "I can't leave. I'm alone in the store."

"How about if I bring something here? Is that okay?" he asked.

Her heart began to pound as it did when Andrew showed his interest in her. She nodded.

"I'll be back in a few minutes," he said as he backed toward the door.

Denise waited in anticipation as Andrew went to the Corner Deli. She'd been thinking about food, but now that Andrew was coming back, food took a back seat to her looking forward to spending an hour with him.

"How's the new job?" she asked as she sank her teeth in the turkey on pumpernickel sandwich.

He shrugged. "It's a job. I have some ideas I'd like to introduce that might make business run a little more smoothly, but I have to wait until I gain their trust first."

"Good idea," Denise said. "No one likes the new employee to come in expecting changes right away."

He nodded. "I remember people doing that with my old company, and I never really respected them."

In spite of his stodgy ways with his sister, Denise saw a lot of wonderful things she liked about Andrew. He was kind, he smiled and laughed a lot, and he seemed to have a good business mind.

After they ate, and in between the few customers who straggled in, Andrew and Denise chatted about everything under the sun. It felt good to be comfortable with a man who was willing to be her friend as well as romantic interest. Her big concern was how he'd react when he found out how much she was helping Amy.

She shoved that thought to the back of her mind, vowing to keep that separate. Her relationship with Amy had nothing to do with Andrew. And vice-versa. But would he see it that way? She doubted it.

"Would you like to do something this weekend?" he asked as they gathered up the papers their sandwiches had been wrapped in.

"I have Jonathan. Bethany and David have asked me to sit with him, and his mother's out of town."

"He can come along," Andrew immediately offered. "I enjoy having kids around."

That was another thing Denise loved about Andrew.

He really did like kids, and it showed whenever he was around Jonathan.

"Okay, but don't fuss at me when I let him get away with stuff," she warned. "I figure as long as he's not getting hurt, he can do whatever he wants with me. I'll leave the discipline to his parents and aunt and uncle."

Andrew held up his hands and grinned. "You can feed him all the junk food you want and let him stay up all night as far as I'm concerned. I learned my lesson last time I opened my mouth."

He said this in a friendly way that let Denise know he wasn't upset anymore. They laughed together, something that felt so good and natural to her.

Amy got her permit with a perfect score on the test. She practically soared all the way out to the parking lot, back to Denise's car. "I can't wait to start driving," she said. "I'll be free, free, free!"

"Try to control that a little, Amy," Denise said, chuckling. She remembered the sense of freedom that getting her own driver's license brought. It was something to worry about.

"I promise I'll behave," Amy said as she tried to stifle her own smile. "But I'm really looking forward to it."

Amy spent the rest of the day talking about all the places she wanted to go once she was driving on her own. Denise listened with great interest. She was finding out things about Amy that intrigued her. Amy really was a fun-loving kind of woman who had a beautiful free spirit.

Denise looked forward to being with Andrew that weekend, although she wondered how things would work out with Jonathan being with them. But Andrew had been so gracious, she couldn't imagine anything going wrong.

The weekend was almost magical. Jonathan enjoyed the male attention from Andrew, and he thrived on sitting between them at the movies. He talked non-stop afterwards, excited about the animated show they'd seen. Andrew acted like Jonathan was the most interesting person in the world, and Denise just sat back and watched. It was wonderful for her, that feeling of things being so right. She didn't want to think about it ending.

After Jonathan went back to David's and Bethany's, Andrew came over to Denise's house and said, "Now I've got you to myself. How about taking a drive over to Plattsville?"

"To eat steak at the Pine Room?" she asked.

He shrugged. "If that's what we feel like doing. But what I had in mind was stopping off at a couple of those little country stores I spotted on the way. It might be fun."

Chapter Twelve

The two of them had one of the best times Denise could ever remember. They talked and laughed about everything under the sun. Too bad it had to end.

As they stood on Denise's front doorstep, Andrew cupped her face in his hands. "You're quite a lady, Denise. And full of surprises, too."

Her heart felt like it was going to jump out of her mouth, it was pounding so hard. All she could do was look up at him and hope he'd kiss her.

"I want to keep seeing you. I've never felt this way with a woman before," he continued.

Denise finally gulped and took a step back. *Would he feel this way after the slumber party*? she wondered. Reality set in fast and hard. "I, uh, better go inside, Andrew. I had fun, too."

He leaned over and brushed a light kiss across her lips, then she ran inside like a crab on the beach. The whole thing was becoming overwhelming to Denise, and she didn't know what to do.

Amy was so excited about the sleepover, she'd abandoned all talk about the driving and spoke of the wonders of being with a group of women all night. "I've always wondered about this," she said. "My parents made it sound so evil."

Denise laughed. "It can get pretty wicked at times, but these women are all grown and respected in the community. We won't lead you astray, I promise."

A quick look of disappointment crossed Amy's face, then the excitement returned. "Oh well, at least I know if you're involved, it'll be fun."

Although she knew people often said things like this, Denise couldn't understand why. All she did was make a few comments and wisecracks, and people laughed. Most people were easy to please, she surmised.

"Uh, Amy," Denise said as she took a step closer to her employee. "Have you told Andrew about the sleepover yet?"

"No," Amy said with a frown. "I was kind of hoping you'd do that for me."

Denise laughed. "No, I'm afraid that's your job. And I don't want to be anywhere near him when he hears about it."

Amy sighed and nodded. "I'll tell him tonight."

That was a good sign. Amy had said she'd 'tell' him rather than ask him. She was growing more and more confident as each day passed.

The next morning, Amy bounced into the store with a huge grin on her face. "I told my brother, and he said it sounded like a wonderful idea."

"He did?" Denise didn't bother trying to hide her surprise.

Nodding, Amy said, "He said it would be fun for me to get to know some other women in town."

Denise let out a sigh of relief. At least he wouldn't read her the riot act now, if he'd had that kind of reaction. Later on that day, he actually came into the store and thanked her. Amy was on break, and she wasn't in the store.

"My sister doesn't do much, and this might be just the thing to bring her out," he said.

Denise nodded, not daring to tell him all the things she had up her sleeve. "Yes, it should bring her out quite a bit," she agreed.

"Since your Friday night is tied up with this sleep-over thing, I was wondering if you'd like to spend a couple evenings with me during the week."

"I'd love to," Denise said with enthusiasm.

When Amy came back from the muffin shop, Denise told her. "And do me a favor, Amy."

"Sure, anything."

"Wait until after this week to tell Andrew about your permit."

Amy chuckled. "Okay. I understand."

Actually, Denise wasn't sure Amy really did understand. All she wanted was a few more nights of magic before the spell was off. She knew that Andrew would consider her a troublemaker after this was all over, but she also knew it was the right thing to do. She'd been torn after she realized she was falling in love with him, but she couldn't let her friend down just because she was Andrew's sister. That wouldn't be fair to Amy, and Denise prided herself on her sense of fairness.

Each time she spent with Andrew was even better than the one before. He was kind and gentle, making her feel special. He gave her his undivided attention, never ignoring her for a single second. And while Denise knew he came from a privileged background, she saw something in him that spoke of understanding and truth, which meant he hadn't been spoiled by all the material things he'd had thrown his way. It was something that had come from deep inside him, which made her love him even more.

The word *love* had always scared Denise. It sounded so permanent, so final. But her feelings for Andrew couldn't be described any other way. She loved him, and at the end of their date on Thursday, he let her know how he felt.

"Denise, I'm falling in love with you," he said softly as they stood on her front porch. "I'm not quite sure what to do about it, though."

She sucked in a breath and slowly let it out. It took every ounce of self-restraint to keep from screaming with happiness. "Let's just take our time and see how things work out."

He backed away slowly, never taking his eyes off her. "Yes, you're right. We have all the time in the world."

If he only knew, she thought. After this weekend, she knew she'd be lucky if he even spoke to her again. As tempting as it was, though, Denise wasn't about to let Amy down. That would be the wrong thing to do.

Amy had brought her overnight bag to work with her since Denise had told her she should just come straight home with her after they closed the store. Her excitement was contagious, and the customers all left the store smiling.

"I can't believe I'm actually going to a sleepover," Amy said over and over in the car on the way to Denise's house. "This is like a dream come true."

Denise smiled and patted Amy's shoulder. "Let's hope you're still saying that this time tomorrow."

"Oh, I'm sure I will."

Bethany was the first friend to show up. Denise had asked her to bring some goodies that she was so good at baking. Turning to Amy, Denise said, "Food is a vital part of a sleepover."

Amy nodded, her eyes still bright. "This is already so much fun."

Bethany glanced back and forth between Amy and

Denise and shook her head. "Just wait, the real fun hasn't arrived yet."

Connie and Phyllis arrived together, their hair and makeup bags dangling from their fingertips. Then, Cindy, Gail, and Linda arrived, all holding platters of fattening and sugary treats.

"Let the fun begin," Denise said as she closed the door behind the last of the guests.

They played music, danced around the living room, and stuffed their faces until they were full. Amy fell right into the groove as she quickly caught on to letting loose and letting her real personality show through.

She told a few jokes that were groaners, but she laughed right along with the rest of them when they threw their pillows at her. "You just don't get it," she said between giggles.

Denise made her way over to Connie and gave her a gentle nudge. "I think it's time now," she whispered.

Connie nodded and moved toward Amy. "Hey, Amy, I've been wondering something."

"What?" Amy asked innocently.

"Have you ever tried anything different with that gorgeous hair of yours?"

Amy frowned. "Like what?"

Denise could sense that Amy was becoming suspicious, so she stepped up to Connie. "Show her something with my hair, Connie. I love it when you fix my hair."

Connie caught on to what was going on. She laughed. "Oh, so you want to take advantage of this party and get a free styling tonight. Well, since you were so generous to invite me, I might as well do your hair."

Everyone watched and egged her on as Connie started out doing absurd things to Denise's hair, then settled on something more realistic. "I love it," Denise said as she looked in the mirror. "Now for the makeup. Got your bag, Phyllis?" She knew Phyllis had it, but she was acting for Amy's sake.

"I never go anywhere without it," Phyllis said with a sly chuckle. Phyllis had a wry sense of humor, and she managed to draw laughter from the way she said things rather than what she said.

By the time Connie and Phyllis were finished with Denise, Amy was jumping around. "Will you do me next?" she asked.

Everyone glanced at each other. This was much easier than anyone had thought it would be.

It only took an hour before Amy looked like a completely different person than when she'd arrived. And she was stunning.

"I can't believe how modern you look," Cindy said, shaking her head. "Your hair is to die for."

"And those eyes," Linda added. "With peepers like those, she'll be able to get any guy in town under her spell. Do me a favor, Amy, and find a man fast so I don't have to compete with you."

Amy was so thrilled with the way she looked, she went around hugging everyone. Denise got caught up in the excitement.

"Why don't I get some of my clothes and let Amy try them on?" she offered.

"Good idea," Bethany said. "I'll bet she's never worn anything like what you've got in your closet."

Denise narrowed her eyes and glared at her in fun. "Watch what you say about my wardrobe, or I'll tell a few of your secrets."

In mock dismay, Bethany shook her head vehemently. "No, please don't do that!"

Amy changed into each outfit and pranced around the room like a runway model. "I love these clothes, Denise! Can I borrow them sometime?"

"Sure," Denise said. "Whenever you want. Just don't tell Andrew where they came from."

The instant she said that, she knew it was the wrong thing to say. Suddenly, Amy's shoulders sagged, and a worried expression crossed her face. "Andrew will kill me if I come home looking like this."

"No, he won't, Amy," Denise said. "He'll tell you to wash your face and change your hair back. Then, he'll come looking for me."

Amy squared her shoulders. "I'm a grown woman, and I can do anything I want with my hair and makeup. No one can tell me what to do."

All the women except Denise cheered. She just sat there thinking about how her own future with Andrew had just gone up in smoke—just because she wanted to be a good friend to Amy. Oh well, she'd been alone before, and she'd remain that way, probably for the rest of her life.

As it grew later and the party progressed, Denise watched Amy as she blossomed into a very social creature, one who loved every ounce of attention she got. "I just love this new hairdo," she commented. "It feels so springy and natural."

"It looks great on you," Connie said, "if you don't mind the artist admiring her own work," she added, giggling.

"And a wonderful artist at that," Amy said as she grinned at Connie.

"Hey, don't forget about the war paint I applied to your perfect complexion," Phyllis said as she nudged her way closer to Amy.

"Of course, I won't forget the war paint." Amy turned to look at herself in the mirror and sighed. "I can't believe the difference."

"What will your brother say?" Cindy asked.

Amy let her head fall back as she said, "Who cares what Andrew says?" Then, she glanced over at Denise, who sat there, taking it all in. Her smile faded. "Oh, Denise, I'm so sorry. I promise I'll let him know that you had nothing to do with this."

"But that would be a lie," Denise said. "Because I had everything to do with this. I told them to bring their supplies."

"I'm glad you did, and no one could do this if I didn't want them to, so don't worry so much." Amy's voice sounded more confident than Denise had ever heard.

They spent the rest of the evening playing picture games and laughing like a bunch of teenagers.

"I can't remember the last time I had so much fun," Linda said as everyone stood at the door the next morning. "We'll have to make this a regular event."

"Sounds good to me," Bethany said. "Next year, we'll do it at my house."

All the women hugged each other, until Phyllis squealed. "Don't look now, Amy, but that handsome brother of yours is heading this way."

Chapter Thirteen

Denise quickly turned toward the direction Phyllis was pointing, and sure enough, up walked Andrew. He had his hands in his pockets, and he looked as though he didn't have a care in the world.

Then, he spotted his sister. At first, he didn't appear to recognize her, but after a few seconds, he realized who she was. He looked confused.

"Amy?" he said as if he couldn't believe what he saw.

"Hi, there, Andrew!" she called out to him. "Like the new me?"

His jaw clenched tightly, he narrowed his eyes and glared at her. Then, he looked back at Denise with an expression she couldn't read. "Andrew?" Amy said. "What's the matter with you?"

"I don't like it," he growled. "Go wash your face."

"No!" she shouted as she stormed past him and headed for his car.

Andrew stood and stared at Denise for a few seconds before he turned and followed his sister back to the car. *Well*, Denise thought, *so much for a relationship with that man*. She knew she might as well forget about her feelings because he didn't appear to be the reasonable man he seemed to be only days ago. And she really hadn't expected him to be reasonable where his sister was concerned.

Denise went inside after everyone had left, and she spent the better part of the morning straightening up. *Now what?* she thought.

She'd already brought one of the part-timers in to work at the store, and she hadn't planned to stop by until later in the afternoon.

Since there wasn't much left to do around the house, Denise decided to head into town and relieve the person who was working. When she got there, the teenager smiled and said, "You must have had a whopper of a party last night. Everyone's been talking about it."

"Really?" Denise said. "Like who?"

She waved her hand toward Main Street. "People are coming from the Cut 'n Curl and saying that your party was the talk of the town last night. Amy must look pretty awesome."

"Yes, she does," Denise agreed. "She looks pretty awesome."

"Uh, Miss Carson, do you mind if I leave a little early? I have a date with Brad, and I wanted to stop off at the mall and pick up a new top."

"Sure, go ahead. That's why I stopped by. I really appreciated your help today. I'll have your check ready by the end of the week."

"Thanks," the teenager said as she practically ran out the door.

Denise stood there and stared at the floor. The sleep-over was barely over, and people were already talking about it. She knew that not much happened in Clear-view, but this was ridiculous. Besides, all they did was talk, do hair, put on makeup, play games, and eat. What was so exciting about that?

Plenty, if you take a meek, mild mannered woman and turn her into a pin-up girl. And now, Denise was back to square one. She had her store, her house, and a few friends. At least she had that, though. It would keep her busy. Too bad a lonely heart had to go along with what she'd done, but she knew it was for the best. If she'd taken the safest route, Andrew might not be mad at her, but Amy would still be in her shell. *This was for Amy*, Denise kept trying to tell herself. Now, who would suffer?

Since the store appeared to be slow, Denise began to pick up all the receipts and stuff them into the night deposit bag. There were a few books to straighten and chairs to move, but that wouldn't take long.

When the bell sounded at the door, she didn't look up right away. A few seconds later, she heard a male clearing his throat behind her.

She spun around. "Andrew?" Her hopes soared.

He glared at her. Her heart sank. Why had she gotten her hopes up that he might find it in his heart to forgive her? Not that she'd asked for forgiveness, but she'd hoped he wouldn't lay all the blame on her.

"Why did you do that, Denise?" he asked, his voice filled with pain and anguish. "I thought I could trust you with my sister."

She closed her eyes. "Trust isn't the issue here, Andrew. Amy has been dying to experiment with her hair and makeup. It was only a matter of time before she sprouted wings."

His lips tightened as he seemed to think about what she'd said. "Maybe so, but she's not ready for this yet."

That was all she could take. Denise placed her hands on her hips and glared right back at him. "Look, Andrew, I would apologize if I thought I did something wrong, but I didn't. Your sister is a grown woman with a mind of her own. I had her as well as a few other friends over, and we just did what women do when they get together."

Andrew listened to her, then shook his head. "I

can't accept that, Denise. And I'm very disappointed in you. I thought you understood."

"Apparently, I didn't," she said softly. "I need to get back to my work, so please either leave or buy a book now."

Denise held her breath while he turned and walked out of the store and out of her life. Her heart felt like it was about to break in two.

The next day at church, Denise saw Andrew and Amy on the other side of the sanctuary. She grinned as she noticed that Amy still sported the new hairdo and the makeup, although it was toned down just a little. *Way to go, Amy*, Denise thought. *At least all this trouble wasn't in vain.*

After the services, Denise left immediately, not feeling much like socializing. She headed straight home.

At first, she thought it was the wind banging a branch against the front of the house when she heard the noise. But it came back again, this time a little louder and with a force so strong it had to be someone at the door.

She didn't feel much like having company, but she went to answer the door, anyway. It was Amy.

"Hi, there," Denise said as she took a step back and let her friend and employee in. "Where's your brother?"

Amy rolled her eyes. "He's out in the car. In case you haven't noticed, he's pretty stubborn." She reached out and took Denise's hands in hers and swallowed hard. "I insisted on stopping by to talk to you for a minute. I hope you don't mind."

Denise managed a short laugh. "I'm surprised Andrew cooperated and drove you here."

"He didn't have much choice. I refused to get in the car with him until he agreed to take me here."

"You're getting good at this new image thing, Amy. Maybe you'd better forget all the things we told you."

"No, never," Amy said. "This is the real me. I'm just glad someone else saw that I had potential. You're a real friend, Denise, and I wanted to tell you how much I appreciate what you've done."

"It was nothing."

"No, that's not true. I know how much you risked to help me. Hopefully, Andrew will see the light eventually, too." Amy glanced at her watch and let go of Denise's hands. "I'd better go. We've been invited over to David's and Bethany's for a late lunch."

"Have fun," Denise said.

"It should be a blast. Gertie's gonna be there. She has a way of making sure everyone is entertained."

After Amy left, Denise went straight to her bedroom, flopped over on the bed, and had a good cry. Everyone was having fun but her. This wasn't normal for Denise at all. What was going on? She'd always been the one who started the fun, but never the wallflower. That sent her back into her deep sobbing personal pity party.

She must have fallen asleep because she found herself being startled awake by another sound at the door. And this time, there was no mistaking that it was someone knocking.

Chapter Fourteen

Denise sat up in bed and rubbed her eyes, daring to take a glance in the mirror. *Eeewww!* she thought. *How disgusting*! She looked like she'd been in a street fight.

But what did it matter? She'd just lost her only chance at true love. Who cared if her eyes looked like someone had left her for dead in a dark alley?

When she opened the door and saw Andrew standing there looking better than ever, she felt like crawling back to her room and pretending she was dead. But she couldn't. The instant she opened the door, he'd taken a step inside. Now he was looking at her, apparently having to hold back a snicker.

"What's wrong with you?" she asked, her voice

whiny. That didn't sound like her at all. What was going on?

"Denise," Andrew said tentatively. "Did I upset you enough to make you cry?"

"No," she said a little too quickly. "Of course not."

"Then, what is it?"

"Oh," she said, racking her brain, trying hard to think of a good reason to have puffy eyes. "I've been thinking about my parents and how much I miss them."

His expression saddened as he reached out and pulled her into his arms. "Oh, Denise, I can only imagine, sweetheart."

Had he called her *sweetheart*? Surely, she must be dreaming.

"I've never had to deal with death of a parent, but I know that if and when that does happen, I'll be devastated." He was still holding her.

"Uh, Andrew," she said, daring to look up into his eyes. "Did you know that you are holding me?"

He quickly let go and took a step back. "I-I'm sorry," he stuttered. "I just thought you might need to be held."

She nodded as the tears began to form again behind her eyes. Even though it was out of pity, she loved being in his arms. "I do need to be held." The problem was, she didn't understand what he was doing here. She was confused.

Andrew reached out, then dropped his arms, looking

totally befuddled as to what he should do. "What do you want, Denise?"

She shrugged. "I'm not sure, but I don't want you to let go of me."

He chuckled.

"It's not funny."

"Denise, honey, I'm not laughing at you. I want to comfort you, and then after you finish talking about your personal grief, I'd like to apologize."

"Apologize?" she asked, the tears suspended from her eyelashes.

"Yes. I was a total and complete fool to have accused you of trying to ruin my sister. She looks good, and I can see that what you did was a marked improvement."

"You can see that?" Denise said with disbelief.

He nodded. "I might be stubborn, but I'm not blind."

Denise thought for a moment and decided to go ahead and tell him everything. She needed to clear the air before they got too cozy. "Were you aware that I've contacted a driving instructor for her?"

"Yes, she told me today." He snorted. "When I first heard that, I almost lost my temper, but Gertie kicked me under the table. She told me I was worse than any overbearing parent she'd ever seen, and she'd seen more than her share in her life."

Denise laughed through the trickle of tears that had fallen. "Gertie told you that?"

"Yes, that among other things. By the time I left, Gertie, David, and Bethany had all taken turns giving me a tongue-lashing like I'd never had before."

"Where was Amy during all this?"

Shaking his head, he replied, "She just sat there and listened. I could tell she was enjoying every minute of it."

"You're not still mad at me?" Denise asked.

"How could I stay mad at the first woman I've ever truly loved?"

"Oh, Andrew," Denise said as she threw her arms around his neck.

He pulled her away but kept her hands in his. "I have one more question for you, though, Denise, so try to control yourself."

Her heart sank. He had a question. It must have been a difficult one because of the intensity showing on his face. She gulped. "Okay, Andrew, I'm ready."

"Denise," he said, then he sucked in a breath. After only a brief pause, he went on. "Will you marry me?"

Her heart almost shot out of her chest. This was the last thing Denise had ever expected to hear. But then, she remembered. "What about Amy?" she asked. "Does she know you're doing this?"

Andrew nodded. "Yes, she knows. I was going to wait until next week and ask you, but she insisted I come over and do it right now. Gertie, Bethany, and David agreed with her."

"They all know?"

Again, he nodded. "And they're right out there in the car waiting to hear what your answer is."

Denise looked into his eyes, in spite of her tears, and smiled. "My answer is yes. I'd love to be your wife." She couldn't believe this. It had to be a dream. Oh well, she figured, she might as well enjoy it until she woke up.

After sealing the proposal and acceptance with a kiss, Andrew opened the front door and motioned for everyone to join them. Amy was the first one at the door.

As soon as everyone was in the room, Gertie announced, "It's about time you settled down, Denise. Too bad I'm not a little younger, though, or I'd give you a run for your money on this guy." She pointed to Andrew with her thumb and raised her eyebrows. "He's cute."

Everyone laughed at her good-natured teasing. And then, Amy hugged Denise. "We'll be sisters now."

Denise was speechless, but she grinned back at Amy. She knew she wasn't dreaming. This was very real. And now, she was part of a family again, and it sure did feel good.